The Wormhole Society

The Wormhole Society

Francis Levy

Cogito
New York

©2025 Francis Levy

Published by
Cogito
New York

All rights and publicity information: philoctates@gmail.com

All rights reserved. No part of this book may be reproduced or transmitted in any form or by any means, electronic or mechanical, including photocopy, recording, or any information storage retrieval system, without permission in writing from the publisher, except brief passages for review purposes.

First printing 2025

Acknowledgements:
I would like to thank Christopher O'Brien
and Michael Dwyer for their expertise, patience, and support.

ISBN: 979-8-9923688-0-2 cloth
ISBN: 979-8-9923688-1-9 paperback

To Arthur Nersesian, Joseph Silver
and all the members of the Monday Writing Workshop

The

Wormhole

Society

1

Fries

It was Saturday night in the East Village and I didn't give a fuck. Noticing the Dominican counterman eying me suspiciously, I upped the ante, stealing a French fry off the top of the cone the woman was holding. Her boyfriend, who sported a Mohawk and had a tattoo of the barrel of a gun on the back of his neck, immediately grabbed the collar of my jacket. He lifted me right off the ground, throwing me down so hard that for a moment I thought my wrist might be broken.

I don't know what made me bend down to retrieve the fry that had fallen to the floor. I quickly bit into it to satisfy an urge whetted by the delectable potato smell that filled the air of the Belgian frites place.

The gash on my forehead was starting to bloody the tiles. I picked up the fry, wiped the blood dripping in my eye, and replaced it neatly on top of her pile. I could see myself on one of the mirrored walls. Tall and thin, I'd been a runner in high school. Now, with my knees locked and my legs thrust backwards, I looked like an ostrich.

The girl had a nice rack which she proudly displayed through her pink tank top. I had made her whole, almost. Stealing a fry from a strange woman is a little like putting your finger under her satin bra strap and gently lifting it. I was aware that for the price I'd already paid, I could have done something else.

"What are you, a tough guy? Are you trying to get wise?"

As Mr. Mohawk feinted threateningly, I was already imagining the repartee, but the couple turned away and were looking at the screen of her cell and laughing merrily about something that had nothing to do with me before I had a chance to respond. So, I was caught off guard when Mr. Mohawk grabbed the scalding hot cone of fries from his girlfriend's hand and shoved it in my bloody face.

They ran across Second Avenue just as the light was changing, disappearing into the crowd in front of the Stage, the East European diner on the other side of the street.

"Fuck your mother!" I shouted.

The expletive was drowned out by a big semi gunning its engine as it shifted gears.

I was now fantasizing about the broad-shouldered Dominican guy, who had breathed heavily while pecking his selections into the terminal. I imagined him performing a wedgie on me as he picked me up and threw me out of the Belgian fry joint.

I wanted to be his bitch. I wanted to be impregnated by him. I wanted to have his kids and live in one of those two-family affairs that you pass on the Van Wyck when you're driving out to the airport.

"The Stroll" is what they call the block that runs on Eleventh Street between Second and Third. By around midnight it was loaded with ladyboys, undeterred by the expensive dirty brick pre-war co-op at the corner with its tony Japanese place, Kanoyama, on the ground floor.

"Goin' out?"

The tranny was ambidextrous, pulling up his skirt with one hand and his tank top with the other.

"Going out?" another whispered through botoxed lips, painted fire engine red. "Looking for a good time?"

I called him Frederick of Hollywood; his balls wagged at me through his stockings and garter belt as he bent over.

"Hey handsome, looking for a date?"

I gazed back when the Hispanic tranny with the pageboy said it and then considered lecturing him about keeping it real.

My downfall came when I started to steal from other peoples' plates.

I plucked my Bic from my pocket and wrote the words down on the back of my index finger, but they smudged almost immediately.

"Hey Sugar!" The black kid with the Diana Ross wig pulled a tit out of his bra and held it out to me.

"Do you have any Nestle's Quik?" I asked in the unlikely event he was lactating.

"This hottie's only quick," beckoned his partner in crime. The partner's enormous hard dick was already creating a tent under his lacy, black slip.

"Can I suck your cock?" He was the rent boy of my dreams.

He picked up his shirt to reveal his perfect tits. Going out with a chick with a dick in comparison to simply going out with a chick is like the difference between ordering a la carte or going to one of those all-you-can-eat buffets.

He wasn't the most beautiful pre-op on the block, but I knew him when I spotted him. He always had his works. He let me twist his nipples as if they were dials, as he shot me up. When we were sitting in our little cove in back of the dumpster behind the St. Mark's Poetry

Project, I loved him more than life itself. And it was all for a good cause because he was going to have the operation. He also happened to be an NYU student (he once even showed me his ID when I evinced some skepticism) so some of the money obviously would go toward his tuition. I've never been good on names so when I cried as I came, I sometimes found myself at a loss for words.

    I've always had a little conflict with the world in that I never saw why my pleasures should have anything to do with you or why yours should have anything to do with me. Who the hell cared who he was as long as he opened his mouth, spread the cheeks of his ass and licked mine? He might not exactly have gotten pleasure from what I wanted, but he knew what turned me on. He knew I loved shame. Pretending he was ashamed and defeated by what I asked him to do, made me hard.

2

Sonya

One of the circulars immediately stood out since it was so different from all the others. It was a cheaply produced glossy with a crude drawing of a ball and chain and then, underneath, a cock.

When the little blue pill no longer helps.

It was a kind of skull and bones for ED sufferers who were mistakenly afraid Viagra caused heart attacks.

**Visit us to take advantage of
our groundbreaking treatment.
Walk-ins welcomed.**

I found it inside a toilet stall at an East Village S&M bar called the Gauntlet. I grabbed it fearing I was running out of toilet paper.

**The Albany Medical Group cannot be
responsible for any pulmonary or periodontal
complications. In a small number of cases**

gangrene can occur, along with psoriasis. Those suffering from Hepatitis C or who experience anaphylactic reactions to peanuts should consult their physician before considering treatment.

Why was an outfit that called itself the Albany Medical Group advertising offices right in the middle of Alphabet City?

I kicked at the snow in front of my feet, using the inside edge of my shoe to make it as difficult for the other tenants of my building as possible.

At night as I heard their screaming kids, their barking dogs, or the self-satisfied grunt of a final thrust come from an open window into our shared alleyway, I hoped they'd die horribly from Marburg's, the human form of bovine spongiform encephalopathy in which the brain turns to mush.

When I got upstairs the heat was just coming on. The clanging of the radiator was like a gavel with the steam hissing malevolently from the valve.

I realized that most people threw these broadsheets in their circular files. Yet I didn't have a choice. I needed to do something before I totally drained my bank account or got killed by an angry tranny carrying a paper cutter—some creature of the night with whom I'd gone too far in my search for a hard-on. But deciding I was going to have one more 24-hours of fun before turning myself in, I called Dial-A-Slave. This service would get you sluts who would do anything for money. Not to deny that I'd always ended up paying the price in every sense of the word. Besides cyberspace, Dial-A-Slave actually had a site on Clinton Street called the Bang Bang Club, where you could redeem American Express Rewards points.

"Strip, bitch!"

She blushed and looked genuinely embarrassed as she pulled down the zipper on the side of her skirt and began to unbutton her blouse. She had an unruly mop of black curly hair and dark swarthy skin. The little fuzz that ran from the band of her panties to her belly button told me that I would soon be burying my face in a soft inviting rug. With her unshaven pussy and big tits, she was the opposite of the anorexic Kate Moss types whose waxed pussies appealed to all the pedophiles in the downtown strip clubs. It was a fucking bummer she didn't have a dick, but as she revealed the furry pelt between her legs, I realized she had the cunt of a '70s porn star. Her hole was the size of a small garage. It reminded me of the awe-inspiring secondary sex characteristics Kim Kardashian had once displayed in her magazine spreads with Kanye West. She had the kind of fulsome tits, ass and snatch that were a dying breed. She still exuded the wonderful feeling that having sex with a stranger was something dirty and even sinful. She was so wayward, fallen and damned that her only possible trajectory was further down. Her watery eyes pleaded for more degradation.

Fuck liberated whores. There was no turning back. I liked them to feel that they had crossed the point of no return when they took money from my hand.

"I wanted a ladyboy, but if you're into extreme humiliation you can stay," I slurred as I cracked a popper and felt a wave of warmth surging through my body.

"I'm OK with it, master," she said in a business-like manner.

"No," she cried, as I reached down and plucked out a couple of her pubes for my collection.

Even though her chest heaved as she whimpered, she was stoic. I imagined that in other circumstances she was the kind of person who employed the expression "I can't complain" when asked about the nature of her condition. You know the type. They're pleasantly lobotomized and always eagerly proclaiming, "Sounds like a plan."

"I'm Sonya."

I figured she must have had some Russian blood. I have a long Russian name that rhymes with Raskolnikov, but people just call me Rusty.

"Nothing like a nice hot golden shower before bed." I pushed her down to her knees and unzipped my fly.

"Say 'I'm a piece of shit.'"

"I'm a piece of shit."

"Say 'I have ugly tits,'" I intoned, as her lips quivered. I could have explained my behavior by saying I was a crazy Russian writer or one of the tormented characters in a Dostoevsky novel, if it wouldn't have taken away the thrill I was getting from her submissiveness. Finding a literary citation and trying to uplift everything by insisting it was art or by mentioning Dostoevsky is just what you don't want to do when you're trying to get your rocks off. Such comparisons might have made Sonya feel better about the maelstrom she was entering, but what good was it going to do me?

"I have ugly tits."

"Say 'I'm a piece of shit' again."

She paused, as if she were wrestling with how far she was willing to go.

"Say it," I demanded.

"I used to think I was somebody, but I'm a piece of shit," she editorialized.

I was so turned on that I had to give her some Sylvester to dance to. I put on "Do Ya Wanna Funk." She wobbled for a second on her platform shoes, climbing atop one of my Naugahyde kitchen chairs, holding her hands in back of her head as she proceeded to gyrate wildly.

"Stick your finger up your ass! How far up is that finger?"

"I can feel a pebble."

I grabbed her wrist. Extricating her finger from her ass, I forced it down her throat.

"Wow, I'm really turned on," she said. "Let's fuck."

"No!" I yanked her off the chair, grabbed her lingerie and clothes from the floor and threw her into the narrow hallway outside my front door, unleashing a cloud of bills into the air like they were confetti on New Year's Eve.

I was afraid she might be whining on all fours outside the door, just like the disturbed young woman I hooked up with on a B&D site. She liked to be dog fucked and had trouble separating after the act.

I got a letter from the managing agent of the building after the couple across the hall discovered the bitch passed out in front of my door. I was creating a dossier and even if I were heading for greener pastures in the multiverse, I still couldn't afford to get into more trouble with the landlord if I wanted to retain my rent stabilized status.

When I looked through the peephole, I breathed a sigh of relief when I saw Sonya was gone.

3

The Wormhole Society

I was sitting in the offices of the Albany Medical Group right down the block from the Hell's Angels. With its fish tank and piles of weathered-looking celebrity magazines, it looked like the waiting room of a dentist's office.

There were people ahead of me: a girl with purple hair, a diminutive black guy with thick glasses who had a case of tardive dyskinesia which led him to constantly lick his lips, a bevy of Orthodox Jews with their long coats and shtreimels and a blond with an uncanny resemblance to a former CNN correspondent, Michelle Kosinski. Were they treating women for ED also? Or had she arrived at Albany in the wake of the rumors about her affair with the British ambassador?

I was waiting for the camera crew to walk in and the little clipboard to pop out announcing "Albany Medical Take 2," but there was just the usual boredom you feel when it seems like nobody is ever going to call your name. The hopelessness was made worse by the fact that there was no receptionist to go up to who was patient and reassuring and told you that your number would soon be called.

I figured it was going to be a while and closed my eyes. I had awakened looking out my window with its rusty accordion window guard and view of the alleyway. Now, for the moment, I thought I might be dreaming. However, I realized I must have bolted from my apartment—even though my leaving was a blank. It didn't add up, but I didn't want to try to make sense of the missing link, which I would have attributed to a blackout if I'd been on anything.

The grim cactus plant that sat on the fire escape across the way could have been the logo for the Hemlock Society. I contemplated simply swallowing a bottle of sleeping pills, until I remembered and reached down for the Albany Medical Group flier with its crude block-lettered typeface.

The flier described the induction process that took place at intergroup headquarters, right around the corner on Third Street. There candidates were evaluated and instructed about "the procedure." After an introduction and evaluation by a facilitator, they were directed to meetings in their respective neighborhoods, if they qualified. It was just the kind of bullshit I would ordinarily have tossed in the garbage.

I had an amyl nitrate headache and ear-ringing tinnitus. Add to that the sharp repetitive beeping sound of a garbage truck backing up, which triggered the part of the brain responsible for both homicidal and suicidal ideation.

I let a little of the dread I was feeling act like a Quaalude, falling into a dream about forced feminization. I pictured myself being dressed up in women's lingerie—lacy bra, garter belt and thong—and then gang raped by a group of men, when all-of-a- sudden I was back in Albany with a woman's voice calling out my name.

"Rusty…Russ."

She was a petite dark-haired Hispanic woman with a big, beautiful ass.

"Russianoff…think Russian with the accent on the second syllable."

"Russian Off." She was choosing the lesser of two evils but still didn't have it right.

My surname is not two words. You have to commit to it rather than try to break it down. I got up, mesmerized by the swaying of her behind. It reminded me of the pendulum on the antique clock in my grandfather's West Side apartment.

"Please take a seat and Jerry will be out to see you," she said when I filled out the usual paperwork concerning my medical history, insurance and primary care physician. There was a whole new crew of people waiting. I figured it was going to be a couple of hours before I saw Jerry.

"If I give you my cell, could you ping me when it's my turn. I might go out for a coffee."

I handed her a fiver.

"There's more where that comes from."

I was still sitting there, rubbing myself through my pants, when she called fifteen minutes later.

"You have a really beautiful ass. I'll let you rub it all over my face. Oh yes, you can sit on my face. I'll be your piece of shit. C'mon baby!"

Even though I tried to make eye contact, the Michelle Kosinski look-a-like turned away, pretending not to hear me, as I talked loudly into my phone.

I didn't even have to wait for my appointment with the facilitator, Jerry Finkelstein. He waved me in as if I were a long-lost relative who he was picking up at the airport. He had a mustache and a toupee and, after he sat me down in front of his desk, immediately began to review my medical history on his iPad.

He was squat and thickly built. I was sure he was one of those tough old Jewish guys who played handball in the parks on the Lower East Side. He was wearing a sweatshirt that read simply "Park East." He sported a pinky ring and gold chain around his neck.

As I tried to talk, he put his hand up like a traffic cop.

"You are about to enter another dimension. A dimension not only of sight and sound, but of mind."

He had uttered Rod Serling's old *Twilight Zone* intro with a straight face.

"It's a secret society that uses wormholes to change people," he announced.

"I came here for an ED treatment."

"I just have to inform you of two risks before we continue: losing the self and ending up lost in time."

"Where does it say anything about this?" I asked.

"No one comes in here on the wings of victory. You don't travel to an alternate universe unless you have to."

I started to feel paranoid. Jerry could be like those repressed memory hucksters who convinced others of untruths through the power of suggestion.

"It's actually quite a bargain," he continued. "There's an infinite number of discounts in proportion to the unending parallel universes. A little like shopping for clothes. You pick one, then another, until the shoe fits the foot. You should try our free introductory offer. You learn all about the wormholes, the society and the meetings. It's all natural and there's no obligation."

Jerry picked up his cell phone, which had been vibrating insistently.

"Yeah, another ED."

He ran his finger down his screen. I could tell he was checking boxes. "Oh, there it is. Yup, uh-huh."

Had he already gotten information about me by virtue of some extracurricular method that was only available to worms?

"You're suffering from a case of terminal uniqueness," he said. "You think you're special, a piece of shit at the center of the universe."

"What are you talking about? You don't know me. I'm not interested in joining anything. I thought I was coming here to get help."

"You're only as sick as your secrets," he replied.

Now I was angry. I thought I was going to the Albany Medical Group for erectile dysfunction. I wasn't interested in hearing some nutjob go on about parallel universes. It was a waste of my time.

"OK, you're in," he said, as he finished typing in some additional comments.

"In what? I wanted help with my problem. What would I have to do?"

"Firstly, you have to start attending The Wormhole Society meetings. Second, you have to find your gateway into the wormhole."

I had no idea what he was talking about. It all sounded like some kind of scam. I never chewed mushrooms. I'd never gone for the mystical trappings.

"Is this a cult?"

"No, it's solitary," he said.

"Solitary? Like where?"

"There's a guy who used to wait in front of that old entrance to the Astor Place subway stop. He just stood there staring at a brick wall. That was his portal. People thought he was nuts. But it's different for everyone. You'll know when you've found yours. Take this for good luck."

He handed me a coin, embossed with the image of a scarab. It read: "Life is a Journey Not a Destination."

Though Jerry could have been one of those medicine men on *Wagon Train* who sold snake oil out of covered wagons, I thought about Virgin Galactic. I could already imagine a closed cabin door and the announcement: "Cabin attendants, please cross check and prepare for takeoff."

The Building

I felt like a dog following a scent. I was having similar impulses. Yet something was standing in the way of my acting them out. It was as if I'd already stepped into my wormhole and gone through some kind of change.

I saw steaming fries sitting on the plate of a nymphet as I walked out of the men's room of the Acropolis, my favorite diner on Avenue B. However, my olfactory sensations were edited. It felt as if I were traveling through a cloud. Was the coin Jerry had given me a talisman? Instead of flying off the handle, I was acutely aware that giving vent to my desires would immediately up the ante.

For a moment, I came incredibly close. Walking by the table, I was ready to snap one up between my fingers. The idea of being caught was delicious. But I could see the writing on the wall that would be the icing on the cake, as it were. Was this what it was like to have a conscience?

My building was on First between Fourth and Fifth. The entrance was right next to the Downtown Cafe, the storefront Mexican takeout place. The smells of onions, peppers, frying meat and melted cheese powerfully beckoned. I meant "gee whiz" but mistakenly blurted out

"Cheez Whiz" to no one in particular. Could this be the gateway Jerry had been talking about?

I never looked at the sandwich board on which the daily specials were listed, since I ate there all the time and was familiar with the tacos, rellenos and burritos. Now I stopped and became totally transfixed. Something that I couldn't exactly identify had grabbed my attention. I experienced vertigo. I momentarily lost my balance. I shook my head when I snapped out of it, sure I'd wrenched my neck.

The staircase groaned from my weight. I could still hear the cries of babies and the sounds of arguing couples and alternating rap and salsa music through the paper-thin walls of the narrow corridors, with their cracking paint and naked light bulbs.

It was a fifth-floor walkup. There were two other apartments on my landing. I had never thought much of the climb. At the price I was paying you couldn't complain, but now for the first time, I was out of breath when I got to the top.

I noticed the tarnished copper cylinder of my lock was now a shiny gold. The jaundiced walls with their chipped plaster had also been painted a mauve color. Was the landlord upgrading so he could evict people like me who paid almost nothing for their rent stabilized apartments?

When I stuck my key in, it didn't fit. There had been times when I was so drunk, I couldn't get in the door. However, I was stone sober now and shivering. I'd been thinking of the hot bath I was going to take. I hit the door angrily with my fist.

"This just isn't my day," I said aloud.

"Who is it? Coming!" a welcoming female voice called from inside. I'd been estranged from my family for years. There hadn't been anyone in my life, after the one disastrous romance of my youth, which after crushing me, led to a life of vengeful sex.

There was a blue-stenciled "5" on the landing. So, I had to be in the right place.

"Coming," she cheerily called out again. I smelled French fries. A beautiful Asian woman with ivory skin and dramatic eyelashes that looked like butterfly wings came to the door. She had plainly just gotten out of the shower. A towel was wrapped around her head. She was carrying a cone of French fries which she immediately pushed in my face.

"Take one," she said.

I shook my head, not knowing what to say to the creature standing in the doorway of my apartment.

"C'mon," she urged.

I again waved the fries away, despite the temptation from the smell now wafting through the hallway.

"Party pooper," she said.

I knew there were a couple of students in the building who had men coming and going at all hours of the night. However, I didn't dare ask her what she was doing in my place and why the lock was changed. We'd just met. I didn't want to sound like the kind of neighbor who's always complaining.

"I guess my coordinates are a little off," I said.

I figured the sandwich board was my gateway. My little comeuppance was part of my first descent. While perusing the society's materials, I read that sometimes these kinds of things happened when you returned from a wormhole.

"I once lived here."

The smile vanished from her face. She pulled the silk robe she was wearing more tightly around her lithe form.

It was not as if she could do anything about it. Yet I was at the same time proud of myself for being so uncharacteristically diplomatic. In my earlier incarnation, I probably would simply have ripped off her towel, asked "wassup bitch?" and walked in.

5

The Downtown Cafe

I walked downstairs and stared at the menu on the sandwich board that stood outside the Downtown Cafe. For a second or two at most, there was nothing. Then I found myself panting and gasping for breath in front of the take-out joint's plate glass window. I figured it was just an anxiety attack. If it occurred again, I'd pop a Xanax.

I felt like I'd accidentally pushed the "delete" button. I was now standing on the opposite side of the street, facing my building, though I didn't remember crossing First Avenue.

I spotted Sonya in the narrow vestibule, studying the names on the mailboxes. I ran into the ongoing traffic without paying attention to what was coming. A cabby blasted his horn and screamed "Faggot!" as he swerved to avoid hitting me. When I got to the entrance, she was gone. Somebody had already buzzed her in.

I followed. Her platform shoes clumped down heavily as she made her way up the steps.

Who the hell else could be availing themselves of the services of Dial-A-Slave this early in the day?

I frantically dug into my pocket for my cell phone and entered the number for the Albany Medical Group.

Your call is very important to us. Please stay on the line. Someone will be with you shortly. This call may be monitored for quality purposes. Please listen carefully as we have changed our options. For English, please press #1. For Spanish, press #2. If you are a health care provider, press #3. For the multiverse, press #4. If you would like to speak to a representative, press #5.

I pressed #4 but after five to ten minutes nothing happened. Feeling like you do after you've had a meaningful dream you're in danger of forgetting, I kept rehearsing the questions I needed to ask over and over: Where was I going? Was there any turning back? Would my medical coverage remain in place even if my identity underwent a change? Would doctors I saw in the parallel universe be considered out-of-network?

I walked back outside, finding myself drawn to the sandwich board for no apparent reason. I already knew the menu by heart. Next to it was an unmarked black door. At first, looking down into the basement area, I thought the floor was moving. Then I realized it was covered with snakes. As I slammed the door shut, there was a flush, followed by the sound of water being sucked down a drain.

Jerry, the Wormhole Society administrator, was still sporting the same "Park East" sweatshirt. His gold chain was nestled on top of thick graying hairs that protruded from his chest.

No doubt about it, monkey business was going on. I went from the Downtown Cafe to the Albany, aka Wormhole Society, without missing a beat. There were times when I awoke from blackouts with strange women in my bed, but in those cases it all made sense due to my inebriated state. I'd been handed a bottle of water on intake into the Society. I needed to find out if it had been laced with something?

Jerry started to say "speak," but there was interference as if another transmission were trying to break through.

Now I felt cramps in my stomach. I couldn't figure out what was happening though every time I started to feel better, I rationalized the interruption much the way people do when they have a brief respite from a chronic illness. Either it was just going to be one of those long days or I was really travelling in uncharted waters.

"Are you crazy?" Jerry asked.

I was beginning to fall down some kind of a chute. "Hold on I have to tell you something…"

I froze up, clinging to the arms of the chair in front of Jerry's desk. When was this going to end? As I was about to talk, I was struck dumb. It was like one of those dreams when you're hitting air. Before I had the chance to get anything out, I found myself again heading toward the entranceway of my building.

I was back in my old place. It was as if nothing had happened at all. I had no difficulty sticking my key in the lock. After wriggling it around as I usually did, it fit perfectly.

Having my old life back was all I could have ever wanted. The reasons why I'd originally sought help were totally forgotten. I was convinced I could control my urges to eat food off other people's plates, along with my need to spend all my money on submissive chicks.

But my happiness didn't last long. The floor started to vibrate. I was sure it was going to give way under me. It felt like an earthquake. I knew I couldn't stay in the building—especially a rickety old wood-framed structure like ours. I dashed down the stairs, running right past the Asian woman with makeup who'd been occupying my apartment. The towel was still wound around her head.

I screamed for her to "stay outta my place."

She regarded me as if I were a psycho.

Once outside it felt like I was coming down from an acid trip. I had a sudden and intense bout of hunger. A discarded carton of Chinese food was sitting on a pile of old *Club International*, the porn magazine that featured chicks with dicks. I dug my hands right into some truly cold sesame noodles. When I was done, seeing no one coming, I crouched down by the side of the dumpster opened the centerfold of a figure who looked like a pre-op transsexual form of Sonya. Figuring the world was coming to an end, I spanked the monkey one last time. I was reminded of 9/11. People had been streaming out of skyscrapers. I relieved my anxiety by jerking off in a packed elevator.

I ran back to the building, stood in front of the sandwich board, heard the swishing sound that I wasn't sure came from inside or outside my head. I quickly swirled into the sinkhole of oblivion.

I had anced that I was now at the beginning of something new. I would be traveling in a way I never had before, but I had no idea of what to expect. Then in a flash, I found my way. It was as if the wormhole had anticipated my thoughts.

I shouldn't have been surprised to find myself in front of Jerry's desk again. He was now reading from a single sheet of paper on which all the options were listed. These were similar to gym memberships where you joined your neighborhood branch or chose the plan that allowed you "full access." I wanted the equivalent of the perks you sometimes got with signing, such as massages, a body fat evaluation and a free tryout session with a trainer. I watched his gold pinky ring as it scrolled down the page to wormholes #1, #2 and #3.

"I think you will be happiest with option #3. It lets you use all our facilities and results in retroactively diminishing payments, as the plan transitions to imaginary numbers."

"I take it there will be a monthly debit and then a 1% credit on my Delta sky miles card," I joked.

Jerry didn't respond. He was apparently an "if you ask the question, you know the answer" kind of guy. "I'll take an aisle seat."

"You don't have to worry about legroom. It's a little like passing through the event horizon of a black hole. You become pure energy. You don't have to worry about taking up space. But there are two things you must remember when entering a wormhole. They come right out of

Hamlet: "To thine own self be true" and "Neither a borrower nor a lender be."

Jerry hit the nail right on the head. What would be the good if I were reduced to a subatomic particle that didn't possess consciousness? On the other hand, if I remained true to myself, how was I going to change?

"OK, this may sound stupid, but what about carry-ons? Do they serve drinks and snacks? I like those blue chips they hand out on Virgin."

You can look at the menu but you don't have to order popped through my brain. I found myself swept up by a force that didn't even give me time to think. It was like one of those dreams where you try to scream and nothing comes out of your mouth.

I was back on the Stroll again, not able to get the taste of oily French fries out of my mouth. It was cold. The ladyboys were out, but I couldn't hear any words coming from their gaping mouths. I knew I wasn't deaf since an SUV cruising the block for action was blasting a track I recognized from Lil' Kim's *Hardcore* album.

I was looking for a familiar face, not because I wanted to fuck anyone in particular, but simply to get my bearings. Then suddenly, as if the mute button were turned off, the sound of their voices came back with a chorus of "Hey, sugars!" "Goin' out?" "Looking for a date?"

It was like putting a shell up against my ear. The cries were the roar of an ocean that would soon sweep me off my feet. The number of hookers increased until they became a mob that threatened to attack. I figured I must be hallucinating when I saw Jerry standing bare-chested, carrying a spear. I cowered and looked for a doorway where I could take cover.

This time my movement through space/time was relatively gentle, perhaps even slowed down. I had the opportunity to dissect what was happening. I was floating through an ether. I figured that parts of the wormhole must be like the eye of a hurricane. I found myself standing in front of the sandwich board of the Downtown Cafe before touching down in Jerry's office. There was a bump, like when the wheels of a plane hit the runway.

I didn't want to give away all my cards. If I told him I had been seeing things, he might refuse to continue the treatment. I'd heard many cases about shrinks who got you off SSRIs or anti-anxiety drugs like Xanax and Klonopin because they didn't want to take a chance with an emotionally unstable patient.

Imagine the malpractice suit that would be filed by someone who landed in the wrong parallel universe—which gave him or her an existence that was worse than the one he already had? I couldn't conceive of descending any lower than Dial-A-Slave, but who knew? The old joke went: *It could be worse, it could happen to me.*

I heard the roar of Harleys pulling up in front of the Hells Angels storefront. There had been several showdowns between the Angels and other gangs. To be initiated as an Angel you had to drink a woman's period blood. Did they take a live-and-let-live attitude towards the innocuous sounding Albany Medical Group? Garbage can lids started to fly. There was crash of broken glass, followed by the sound of sirens.

"Roll down the gate!" Jerry yelled. "Go out the back way."

It didn't seem to matter since I had already gone out and come back without even bothering to get up from my chair.

The World Trade Center

It was hard to accept I had gone anywhere when my feet were planted solidly on the ground. However, suddenly, I found myself in a new and better form of mass transit that didn't involve delays or stoppages before a subway pulled into a station. There was no waiting on the tarmac. All the drawbacks of being an object with mass were instantly removed.

I was standing in front of the sandwich board again, scouring the menu. Time travel was zapping the energy right out of me. I was starving. Rolling my eyes down the list of the day's specials, I knew the vegetarian enchilada was just what I'd been looking for. There was something magnetic about what was happening to me. It was like the way metal filings on a worktable are magically swept up by a force.

I opened my eyes and, holy cow, I was elsewhere! How did I get here?

"Hey you! You have to go to the security desk." I recognized where I was right away. It was the lobby of the Deutsche Bank building where I'd gone right before the plane had crashed into the World Trade Center.

"What's the date today?" I said out loud. I looked at the digital clock on the ticker running along one of the walls that gave stock prices.

"September 10th?"

"No, it's the 11th."

"Oh, shit!"

I'd been on my way to a job interview before the attack had brought the city to a standstill.

The guard pointed to the center of the lobby where three attendants wearing earpieces were checking IDs and issuing building passes which activated the electric eye on the turnstiles.

"Where are you going?" She was a heavyset woman, who didn't even look at me as she checked my license.

"I don't know."

"Just give me the name of the company. I'll locate the floor."

I just stood there, unable to ask the question.

"It'll be on fire by the time I get there."

"What!

Suddenly everything became blurry. I was starting to go off again.

The tall black kid wearing sunglasses and oversized earphones, who had been standing behind me in line at the security desk, intoned *Motherfuckers wanna test me, wanna arrest me.*

I experienced temporary amnesia. I couldn't remember my own name. You're getting rusty, I thought. I went through all the possibilities...Rudolph, Rudy...Rusty! It was very much like loading your old hard drive into a new computer and the files start to be displayed on a once virgin screen. I immediately understood who I was. The configuration of the lobby was already slightly altered.

People forget names all the time. That was nothing unusual. It was my continuing guilty feelings towards Sonya that gave me pause. The fact I had gone too far created the most direct connection to the universe from which I'd come. She was a good kid who simply hadn't realized her potential as a bitchy slut. Who needed Jerry and his stupid Wormhole Society? You don't experience gratitude until the life you've been living is taken away. Now I just had to make sure my name was removed from their mailing list. I didn't want the fireworks or any of the other side effects that came with it.

"You need to see someone."

Jerry suddenly materialized before my eyes. It was as if he'd been monitoring my thoughts. I wasn't even standing in front of my usual takeoff point, the sandwich board. His springing into my consciousness out of nowhere worried me. I apparently remained in the net. The spell hadn't been broken. You had to be careful what went through your mind when you were in the wormhole.

"You should check if wormhole therapy is covered under COBRA," he said, "which is provided by health plans for dismissed employees. And you still have to sign our liability form. It isn't any more dangerous than crossing the street, but we must make sure we're protected before we send you off on your next adventure."

I had another three months left on my COBRA, but I never checked whether I would still have coverage if I became someone else in a parallel universe. In any case, the policy only covered ten visits.

I didn't have the balls to argue with Jerry. I might not have liked it, but I'd really gotten somewhere.

Something must have tripped a switch. Was it a rush of desire that brought back the memory of Caesar's Retreat? The massage parlor had been on the mezzanine of the old Commodore Hotel, above Grand Central, a building demolished in the early '80s to make way for the Grand Hyatt. The receptionist wore an embroidered toga and a gold band around her head. She had frightened eyes and smudged mascara. Her voice quivered nervously as she explained the three plans: the Caligula, Plato's Retreat and the Academy.

"Holy crap!"

I suddenly found myself wafted to the Forum in ancient Rome. How did I get here? Gladiators were spilling blood. I felt like I was viewing myself as an outside observer, but there was nothing I could do. My mind was playing tricks on me. I obviously wasn't totally aware of what was going through my brain, but I was sure it was driving the show.

Now pretty eunuchs with high voices were fetching voluptuous women from the fishbowl, the glass enclosed viewing space in Thai brothels where numbers hung from girls' necks.

I was experiencing vertigo. I was in Jerry's office again. What the hell happened to ancient Rome?

"The first bite is the banquet," Jerry said.

I fell through the floor.

"You're actually good at this, but you're all over the place. Too much mentation. You have to learn to stop yourself from going off or you'll keep changing channels.

The rest of his words became inaudible as I stepped into a free fall. Once I got past the feeling of jumping from a high dive—where your stomach feels like it's going up into your head—I enjoyed the force of my own inertia. Though I was falling, I had the illusion I was flying because the descent never came to an end.

I shuddered as I returned to where I'd been.

"You're still fighting it," Jerry said. "I'm talking to the Rusty in the here and now, but what Rusty will I be speaking to in two days?"

I felt defensive. I wanted to tell him he was wrong.

"This isn't the usual thing where you set a goal for the March of Dimes fundraiser and try to meet it. Know what I'm saying?"

I found myself back in that packed elevator I'd squeezed into in my panic to get out of the building back on 9/11. I was buffeted along by a crowd of people. I panicked as you do when you're rolled by a wave.

In the middle of it all, I thought about the menu of specials on the sandwich board outside the Downtown Cafe. I found myself home again on safe ground.

I had once tried to create a gloryhole experience with my Electrolux. Luckily, I removed my dick before I got hurt. This is what wormholing felt like to your whole body. So, I had a frame of reference when it came to pulling out of a fall.

For instance, let's say I wanted to get into a parallel universe in which today was yesterday. I had to basically stop myself before I even got started. It was a little like trying to brake while a car was skidding or "edging" in the course of masturbation.

Once you got the hang and weren't all over the place, you could zero in on wherever you wanted to go. You could eliminate ED and produce all the other good things that went along with living in a parallel universe. But you had to watch out since any thought going through your head could end up propelling you into the nether reaches of one or another eternity.

I entered my wormhole by standing in front of the sandwich board outside the Downtown Cafe, with its daily advertisements for Cocina Mexicana.

However, I needed to know more before bungee jumping into oblivion.

I called my insurance to see whether I was still eligible for wormhole therapy. I spoke to an operator in New Delhi by the name of Shakti, who reassured me the COBRA plan I got on after I was fired from my last job teaching ESL to cemetery workers provided for ten sessions of PT under the diagnostic code, which dealt with out-of-network or, in this case, multiverse claims.

I should have known what the deal was but when I worked for the union, I spent most of my time avoiding the president, Dan Fogarty. A bruiser with mob connections, he had a reputation for bonking everyone in sight and was constantly giving me the evil eye.

7

The Meetings

I was still so out of sorts, I had no problem getting the motivation to attend the Wormhole Society. After you were discharged from a rehab like Hazelton you went to AA. The WHS was a natural progression from the Albany Medical Group.

My first meeting was in the basement of the Church of the Earthly Resurrection, which was right down the block from the Bang Bang Club. It was a storefront that also provided a performance space for the vestiges of '60s avant-garde performance groups like the Theater of the Ridiculous and the Living Theater, which had just staged an all-nude performance of *Paradise Now* in the same basement level space where the Worms met.

As I took a chair, an animated fight had just begun between several members about whether to take down one of the group's posters that depicted a naked woman with a laurel wreath in her hair. A pushing and shoving match broke out when a transgender female with fake eyelashes tried to stop a heavyset butch with tattooed biceps and a crew cut who tore the poster as she peeled it from the wall.

I made an about-face when I spotted a number of trannies I'd fucked sitting in a semi-circle of metal foldup chairs.

In the Wormhole literature they tell you to avoid people, places and things. Here I was heading into the eye of the storm. In a panic I made my way back up a narrow stairwell that smelled of urine.

I stopped in my tracks when I saw Sonya. At first I thought she was simply another one of those peasant women with the babushka tied around her chin who man the counters at the Ukrainian restaurants on the Lower East Side. Then I did a double take. Due to the outfit and the absence of the studs in her eyebrows and nose, lips and tongue, I hadn't recognized her.

I could hear her telling her story to a woman with spiked hair and a tattoo on her face whose eyes were red from crying. As the two passed right by me, I stupidly waved, not sure whether she'd register who I was or not.

"The guy who just walked by us nearly destroyed me." She raised her voice loudly as she made the accusation.

I hoped there was someone else with whom I could be confused but the stairwell was otherwise empty. I didn't know much about the protocol, but I was taken aback by the attack even considering all that had gone on between us. I thought I'd be welcomed even by those I abused. I was not a bad person, as the literature said, I was a sick person trying to get better.

I'm sorry for everything I did to you, and I promise to pay you back for all those bills I threw over your naked body. I had already rehearsed what I would say to her, if I ventured into a meeting and saw her. But the words were stuck in my mouth.

"Easy does it," she said to the woman I assumed was also a new recruit. They continued down the steps. "This is a great meeting and it's very small so everyone gets to share."

But I'm terminally unique. No one will understand my problems, I thought as I followed them. There was no way I was going to join some group of flunkies. Was I trying to deal with my problems or was I just looking for trouble? I had no intention of going along with any of this shit. Yet I had nowhere else to go. Despite the pain I was lured back by Sonya and the memory of the scene of my crimes.

When I walked back down to the basement, I noticed that the whole room was filled with whores who had migrated from the adjacent coffee nook and were now reading aloud from some kind of book.

When the reading was over, Sonya took the mic and said, "I'm Sonya and I'm a Worm."

"Hi Sonya," the others intoned.

"I am now proud to introduce our own Tiffany."

I recognized Tiffany right away. She was an infamous East Village institution, a slut who had been permanently 86'd from the Bang Bang Club for giving it away free.

"My name is Tiffany. I'm a Worm."

"Hi Tiffany," the group intoned.

"Men, women, I could never get enough and when I realized I could profit from my addiction, I was off to the races. One time I OD'd, but wouldn't you know it, I ended up sucking off the attending physician in the ER after he pumped my stomach. When I was too fucked up on crank to sell it, I let them do anything to me that they wanted. That's how I got the starring role in *Stretched Thin*. But once I started to attend the meetings and learn the ins and outs of the wormhole, I began to live a life beyond my wildest dreams.

"Sure, the first place wormholing landed me in was ancient Rome, where I attended one of Caligula's orgies. I also went to the Marquis de Sade's hometown Lacoste, becoming one of his servant girls at the height of his infamy. Little did I know that I would run into a later incarnation of him at Wormhole Society meetings. However, I was also a pterodactyl, one of the flying reptiles that roamed the earth before the ice age. I was there for the building of the Pyramids and the Taj Mahal and actually hitched a ride on Halley's Comet. Now because of this wonderful program, which has allowed me to travel through space and time to parallel universes where I'm able to be discover my best self, I've become happy, joyous and free."

I was staring at Sonya, secretly hoping that she would glance in my direction and acknowledge my existence. She looked devout, her eyes welling up with emotion behind her babushka. After the cold shoulder she gave me, I seriously thought about trying to get her to blow me in one of the stalls of the church bathroom. I'd submit the iPhone video to SexinPublicPlaces.com.

Why was I thinking these things when I was on my way to some parallel universe where I was supposed to be a different person? They say once you become a Worm, you can never be a butterfly. Getting trashed and having angry sex would never be the same. But I still was pissed at her holier than thou attitude. I hated it when reformed sluts took on spiritual airs.

You have to forgive before you can ask forgiveness. I came upon the line accidentally after thumbing through *Worms*—the big black book I knew to be the bible of the society. I didn't exactly understand what the words meant, nor did I have any intention to act on them. However, they made me think as I entertained the prospect of testing Sonya's gag reflex in the men's room stall. Sure, I was all for it, if I could mouth a few phrases and test my plumbing out on Sonya's mouth.

"I think I will wrap it up by saying that if you're new, keep coming back. If you've been around for a while, try to remember that it's not a self-help program or a program of self-improvement. If you can't give it away, you can't get it. Travelling billions of light years is a trip, but it ain't tripping."

I noticed a few Worms looking at each other like they weren't understanding what Tiffany was getting at.

"Thanks so much, Tiffany. That was really great. Are there any newcomers here for the first time, who would like to introduce themselves?"

I was sure Sonya was going to look in my direction, but she just kept staring straight ahead.

"OK. Is there anyone working on ninety days or an anniversary of a year or more?"

No hands went up and I figured I would just disappear into the crowd after the meeting was over. No one would care whether I came or went. Sonya scanned the room once again. I was sure she saw me, but she refused to acknowledge my presence even as we made eye contact.

Suddenly, as if propelled by an involuntary movement, my hand shot up. The butch who had been fighting about the poster shouted out, "We have a newcomer who wants to introduce himself."

"I'm Rusty and I've already been Rudy depending on my level of quantum entanglement and my position in the multiverse."

I knew I was trying to impress. The minute the words came out of my mouth, I also knew it was hopeless. I felt my dick scrunching up the way it does when I am nervous—like the head of a tortoise receding into its shell.

"Hi Rusty or Rudy," the others chanted.

I wasn't sure where my words were coming from, though such prima donna-like behavior is what cornholers like me are all about! I am special and different. I hang on to the image of James Dean in *Rebel Without a Cause*. The great I am. No one understands. The rules don't apply to me.

My provider offered a list of in-network wormhole therapists. The one I ended up choosing was a Rastafarian Jew whose parents had named him Cliff (after Jimmy Cliff) and who talked with a heavy Jamaican accent even though he'd grown up in Scarsdale. He worked out of the Flatiron branch of the YMCA. The rehab area was in the basement next to the room where the spinning classes took place. You could hear the instructor exhorting his students to push their aerobic thresholds to a state of breathlessness.

"If you get off your bike and feel like you can walk and think rationally, then you're kidding yourself."

"When you were a kid did you ever think you could jump out the window and fly?" Cliff asked.

I thought for a moment before answering.

"Yeah, I think that was right before they put me on Ritalin."

"You gotta look right out that window and imagine you have wings," he said.

The darkened window in question was on the sub-basement level of the gym. Yet I nodded as if I understood what he was talking about.

"Look, pretend you're in a writing class at the New School or one of the online sites that advertise continuing ed courses in acting. They're the court-of-last-resort, right? Everyone who's in a dead-end job or relationship thinks about taking 'Writing from Experience' at the New School. That's what it's like negotiating these wormholes. It's somewhere between jumping out a window and taking creative writing at the New School. You have yet to hit rock bottom. You must know in your soul that there's nowhere else to go."

"I'm a little worried that the only way I'm able to get into the wormhole is to stand in front of the Mexican restaurant outside my building. There are sandwich boards that gives the day's specials."

"I wouldn't beat yourself up about that. That's an asset. You've found your portal. Once you arrive in a dimension that contains one of the infinite mutations of your being, a process occurs called *melding* whereby your identity is simply subsumed to your destiny.

"I'm going to have to get used to this."

"That's what we're here for."

Cliff began to waltz around the room, flinging his arms up and down as if they were wings.

I spread my hands out and proceeded to leap. The wood floor had been polyurethaned and I almost skidded into a Pilates reformer.

"You look like you're beginning to get the hang of it." He looked blankly at me.

I raised my arms and found myself upright again.

Cliff had turned away to field a call. Like a cartoon character, I was constantly morphing in and out of my varying selves.

The Breakup

I was surprised when I heard thunder then rain pelting the windows—since it had been so beautiful out less than an hour before. The phone started to ring. Instinctively I began to look for it when I realized that unless my cell was suddenly making the sound of a ringing landline, there wasn't supposed to be a black mausoleum-shaped telephone in my apartment.

I was frantic to figure out what was going on, since it was the only inkling I had that everything might not be back to normal. Suddenly it stopped. I figured the ringing had come from an adjacent apartment. Then, just as I was trying to console myself with this rationalization, it started again, even more insistently, as though it were coming after me like a heat-seeking missile.

I finally spotted an old rotary phone that looked like a miniature cash register. A shiver of fear ran through me. Had I yet to return from where I'd been? I was momentarily being detained at some place in the past. It was as if I'd come only part of the way back to my present.

I picked it up and curtly asked, "Who is it?"

There was a silence. I could hear a car honking in the background, so I knew someone was on the line.

"I want to end the relationship."

The woman's voice was on the tip of my tongue but I couldn't place it, no matter how hard I tried to scour my past depredations. She uttered a few more words, but a vacuum cleaner which had started up in the background was coming closer, making it difficult to figure out what she continued to say.

Whoever it was, I remembered the aversion I once felt for her sententious, self-dramatizing tone. It was someone I'd literally known in another life decades before, someone I'd fucked a couple of times, then dumped. She was ending up on top by getting the last say. But who was she? And why was this person, whose name I couldn't remember, calling now?

"I think you have the wrong number," I said, just as the vacuuming stopped. I could hear breathing on the other end along with more sounds of cars honking and then a click, leaving only a dial tone.

Everything was the same except for the phone—and the call.

I lit out of my apartment, running through the narrow hallways and jumping five and six steps at a time. Screaming to a halt in front of the Downtown Cafe, I fell into a panic when I saw that the sign was gone.

"Where is your sandwich board?"

I tried to be as nonchalant as possible. I held my own hand to control my shaking,

"No entiendo."

He put his hand up and went into the back and a few moments later an older gentleman with a shaved head and gray moustache emerged from the kitchen.

"Your board's broken? Wanna sell it?

"No thanks. I sent Jorge around the corner to get a new hinge."

He wasn't giving any credence to my request, but this was the Lower East Side. My desperation was plainly whetting his appetite.

Shit! Had he found out about the sign? Was he going to become like a travel agent who collected commissions? Right now, he had a captive audience. Was he going charge me for my trips into the wormhole?

Even though I could try to visualize the sign, I sometimes got a weak connection. I had to go to his sandwich board if I really wanted to be sure I was getting anywhere. Who knew how many other people depended on this particular carrier—which as far as I was concerned, at least for now, was the only show in town.

"Listen, I'm a carpenter," l lied. "Can I fix it for you?"

I had to correct my course, so I took a seat at one of the oilcloth tables and ordered the chile rellenos plate which came with yellow rice and refried beans. While I was waiting for my food to come, I picked up a copy of the *New York Post* which was lying on a nearby table, comforting myself with yet another front page story about Kim Kardashian.

I was so lost in my reverie that I didn't notice the young woman with slightly pockmarked cheeks sitting opposite me. She was wearing a revealing plaid shirt and black Converse sneakers without laces. She also reminded me of someone I couldn't immediately place.

"Javier," I called to the short order cook in the back. "I'll be right back."

I bounded up the stairs. The phone was still ringing as I got my keys out, but then it stopped. When I got downstairs, the girl, whoever she was, was gone. The sandwich board, with today's specials, had been returned to its usual spot outside. It was like a glitch in a computer. A program may not be working, but all of a sudden resets itself and you're in business. I stood before the sandwich board. Like in Monopoly, I was back at Go.

I returned to my apartment and, sure enough, the phone was gone. I was again like most people who saw no need for a landline. I was comforted knowing I was in my old life. Would simply going to the meetings be enough? Would I need something more?

Downstairs in the restaurant, I caught myself when I saw another young woman in a revealing tank top plucking a stringy piece of melted cheese from her nachos. I still hadn't lost the desire to stick my fingers in her pile.

I listened to the banter of a pair of cops whose squad car was parked at the curb. One was telling the other the old joke about the guy who dies and then is reincarnated. In his new life he's become a bull in Minnesota. My experience had made me a quick study. After overhearing it, I wormholed into a bull—with my life reduced to sleeping, fucking and eating grass. Luckily, I was able to conjure up the magical mysterious sandwich board, finding myself again outside my building.

I remembered the "do the next right thing" homily from the one meeting I attended and headed off to the Church of the Earthly Resurrection. I was hoping I would find Sonya, but I didn't see her. I put my hand up on several occasions. Unfortunately, the speaker, another woman I thought I remembered from Dial-A-Slave, seemed to be calling on anyone but me.

I was suspicious, but I felt impelled to get recognized, simply because I was being rejected. I could have been standing outside the velvet rope at some downtown club, with a bouncer pretending he didn't see me.

When it was over I walked off alone, as the rest of the group talked gaily, bragging about their wormhole trips, even just to Rome or Ithaca, New York.

Successfully imaging the board again, I slid back into the wormhole and found myself in the middle of a conversation I'd had with Jerry only a week before.

"So I told her if you don't like eggs, why do you always order the omelet?"

He was illustrating one of his spiritual axioms.

It was like having a large archive of past and future conversations at my disposal. They say that a therapist only wants to be one or two steps ahead of his patients, but there's nothing to stop the pigeon who can navigate a wormhole from getting access to insights that might otherwise have been years away. The only problem is that you're going to reject everything you're not ready to hear.

That was the thing about parallel universes. You didn't have to give up your life. You could have it all in a slightly modified form. It was a little like gene editing with CRISPR, and there was no waiting for subway trains that were being delayed "due to an earlier incident."

Imaging the sandwich board, I found myself back at what was plainly another version of the same meeting. Sonya was standing by a seat in the front row. She wasn't wearing the babushka. Her jet-black hair, pulled tightly back, accentuated her ivory skin. It looked like she had some kind of spiritual awakening. Now, instead of covering herself like a woman in mourning, she was letting it all hang out. She wasn't even wearing a bra. My mouth watered as I stared at her hardened nipples, poking through the novelty T-shirt she wore.

I might have been a defendant at a war crimes tribunal at the International Criminal Court. Except that all of us were there for the same reason. We weren't bad people; we were sick people trying to get better.

I decided to take a chance. I walked over to her. However, when I got close, she turned away and continued to talk with another woman who I remembered from a very hot video called "Anal Plug."

My face grew red hot with shame and embarrassment as I stood there being ignored when, suddenly, I began to levitate. I felt my feet rising from the ground as I was sucked into the wormhole again.

My heart pounded. I realized I hadn't known happiness until I felt the key slide into the lock and turn the cylinder. There, laid out before me, was my musty apartment with its box of handcuffs, dildos, and stacks of old issues of *Hustler* and *Club International*. Nothing had changed. On the kitchen counter, the browning core of an apple had been left in the ashtray with a roach. A serrated edge knife encrusted with bits of ossified peanut butter lay in the sink.

The Diner

I thought about Sonya's nipples as I ogled the steaming onion loaf through the window of Dallas BBQ, the rib place on Second Avenue. Passing by, I had the urge to shove my fist right through the window. I wanted to rip off Sonya's dress. I could see the buttons flying in the air as her breasts popped out like a pair of bull's eyes sizzling in a frying pan. That would wipe the beatific look off her face. I imagined her downcast eyes opened wide with a mixture of horror and excitement.

As in a fairytale, I would be the prince freeing the beautiful Rapunzel from the tower. I knew that Sonya wanted to get down and dirty.

I was sleeping, as I often did at meetings—now that I attended regularly—when I was shaken awake. I was about to strike back. I figured I was snoring, and that some self-righteous shit was going to 86 me. Luckily, I didn't let go of my hands…it turned out to be Sonya. Her eyes were impassive, with no hint of hate or love. It was almost as if she were unfriending me on Facebook. Even though I was being hypervigilant about my conduct, as if I were walking on glass, she seemed totally unselfconscious.

"We're going around the corner to the Acropolis for coffee, do you want to come?"

"Sure."

I felt hesitant in the way I hadn't in years. I hated her for being so standoffish and upright (I remembered when she said "Yes, master"), but I also wanted her more when she was playing so hard to get.

Ten minutes later, I found myself sitting in a booth between Sonya and Tiffany. They were in the middle of an animated discussion about the varying wormholes they had traversed—taking the very first Hajj to Mecca, or witnessing Halley's Comet sweeping across a night sky in 1066 right before the Norman Conquest. Of course, all I could think of was the great sandwich they would make with their nude bodies pressing up against me.

"It's so cute," Tiffany said, describing her portal, a little crack in the sidewalk in front of the Con Ed power plant on Avenue C.

"It's like a popper. My face flushes. The next thing I know I'm chasing beaver with Sergeant Preston in the Yukon."

"I use the sandwich board on which the specials are listed in front of the Downtown Cafe," I interrupted excitedly, regretting having given away my little secret. Portals were like broadcast frequencies, which could be overtaxed during hours of high demand. I was afraid of rush-hour traffic.

Sonya and Tiffany glanced at each other like they knew something I didn't. Was I going into the wormhole that was used by all the perverts and pederasts? Even though wormholes were supposed to be personal, these kinds of fears were frequently discussed at the meetings. The notion that wormholing could be exploited by media giants like Rupert Murdoch was also a constant subject of discussion. Everyone at the meetings knew you had to hit a bottom before anything would happen, but there were constant worries that Facebook and Twitter would eventually find ways in for their subscribers.

"I'm working with Jerry and Cliff, so I have my choice of portals, of course."

Naturally I was lying. Neither told me where to go. I just stumbled into one because it was in front of my house. From what I could see, a wormhole is a very personal matter. These wormholes are almost like placebos—you have to want them to work for them to be effective. And only you can find your wormhole. Once you do, no one else can use it.

I hated myself for feeling the need to interrupt them. If I'd been more confident, I would have been able to sit with my discomfort.

Four other Worms were already in the diner. When we arrived, the owner moved two more tables over to accommodate our party, which I realized with its bedraggled group of apostates was a kind of perverted Last Supper. And all Sonya would have needed was a baby and a manger to look like a not so virgin-looking Mary.

I regretted consenting to come from the moment I sat down. Why had they even invited me? People at the meeting were always saying, "Take the cotton out of your ears and put it in your mouth." They had no interest in what a newcomer had to say. But looking around, I noticed we weren't the only group in recovery. I saw people all over the restaurant holding hands and quietly intoning the serenity prayer. The Acropolis was a big KA—Kleptomaniacs Anonymous—hangout too. This explained why the salt and pepper shakers had been removed from the KA tables. I wondered if the KAs would perform an intervention on me if I stole some fries?

A lot of the qualifications at Wormhole meetings are really self-degradation-a-logues culminating at the moment a Worm finds their wormhole and is finally set free from the bondage of self. But my problem with the meeting was after hearing a girl or ladyboy's bukkake experience, I'd end up so turned on that I had to do everything in my power to stop myself from heading over to the Bang Bang Club.

"The thought of sucking guys off through a hole in the wall still turns me on," Tiffany was saying.

"Glory hole," I muttered sagely.

"I pray," Sonya said, undoing a barrette and shaking free her hair. It was as if she had been dead and was now reborn as the Clairol girl. "I know my higher power is looking after me."

I picked up the menu and ordered the fried chicken basket. It was advertised as coming "nestled in a bed of sizzling fries," but I told the waitress to hold for a second when I noticed that everyone was staring at me.

"Do you really need all the fat and carbs?" Tiffany asked.

I had to get the hell out of there. What more did they want? I had given up stealing and humiliating prostitutes and now I couldn't even have French fries when I was willing to pay for them.

"I'll change my order, when the waitress comes back."

"Server," Tiffany corrected. "I remembered when I was first coming around how hard it was. Every good-looking guy was a stallion. I spent most of the meeting having fantasies about mounted policeman and the way their horses lowered their huge cocks into the gutter when they were about to take a piss. I was in love with a horse as a kid. I cringed when those poor horses were cut proud."

Tiffany had a far-away look. While she was at a loss for words, she was also plainly not ready to relinquish the floor.

That's probably why I wasn't getting called on. I was an open wound.

They'll get you drunk before you get them sober was an old AA expression that Worms often used when they were trying to figure out how to deal with newcomers.

Don't compare your insides to someone else's outsides.

Tiffany, like a lot of women I have known, was obviously trying to come to terms with her adolescent attraction to horses. I don't think I've ever heard a better description of penis envy. She and I have one thing in common. We can't keep our eyes off tail. If I were to take a detour and do a little more "research," as people in the meetings called it when you had a slip, Tiffany would be the perfect person to go to the Bang Bang club with.

"I'll have the steamed lentils with an order of Greek yogurt on the side," I said when our "server" returned. I practiced getting rid of my stinking thinking by remarking to myself that "they" (I remembered that "she" is out) had a pronounced behind which could be a sign of encroaching obesity (and even diabetes).

"Do you want a basket of bread or rolls?" the waitress asked.

I could see Sonya looking out of the corner of "their" eye, as if to dare me.

"No, I'll just have a side order of the collard greens."

My face flushed. Suddenly, I felt the rush. I knew the feeling immediately. I figured I might have entered someone else's wormhole by accident. I'd just read a story about a guy in Sarasota who had fallen through a sinkhole right in his bedroom when the floor caved in. So, there was no reason I couldn't have been staring at the right place at the wrong time.

It was like the feeling of one of those water slides at Six Flags. I heard a whooshing sound as I slipped out of the present, finding myself lying on the couch in a psychoanalyst's office.

"Well, we have to stop," she said.

Her office radiated culture. There were copies of *The New Yorker*, *The New York Review of Books* and even *The Times Literary Supplement* in her waiting room. On the wall facing the couch, on which I lay, was a framed poster from a Joan Miró show at the Galerie Maeght in 1953. When I got up I looked out of large French windows facing a tree-lined street. It must have been late spring, the leaves were in full bloom. Across from my analyst's office stood a red brick Georgian building with white molding. Schoolgirls in tartans were pouring out for recess.

Now that I was beginning to know my way around, I was aware that most wormholes involved time travel. However, I also realized that within this new parallel universe, which was very close to my own present coordinates, I'd had a very long and unsuccessful analysis. Many of the sessions were used for describing how I acted out with prostitutes or cheated on the woman with whom I was cheating on my wife.

Termination was the subject. When was I going to end the misery? When would I finally grow tired of reporting how sullied I felt from my latest episode administering punishment to some sad creature who would do anything to support their drug habit? When would my obsessions with shit, urine and cum cease?

"There's a price to be paid for everything," she said (I knew that being an old-fashioned therapist she would have been comfortable with my using traditional pronouns) after I described the old days of the slave auction at the Hellfire Club.

"But maybe it's worth it."

She said nothing else for the rest of the session and neither did I.

One sure way to terminate was to climb right back in the wormhole from whence I came—though why would I want to give up being a wealthy stock trader, who had the money to use exclusive services like the one that had been the downfall of the governor of New York, Eliot Spitzer, The Emperor's Club VIP?

I decided to go back to the Park Avenue apartment I had been allowed to keep in the settlement with my third wife, who it turned out had been outdoing me at my own game by sleeping with the butcher, the baker and the candlestick maker, in addition to the gardener and all our friends. I intended to crack open a bottle of Cristal and think about what I really wanted before deciding to give up all the perks of this particular parallel universe.

When I got into the apartment I stared admiringly at my winnings, which included a pewter vase filled with freshly cut flowers and a Keith

Haring drawing. I pulled my Emperor's Club VIP card from my pocket and dialed the number on it.

I didn't want to get into trouble with the board. Still, these girls were presentable. They could easily be mistaken for art dealers, interior designers or even wealthy investors in my fund. You don't get the kind of whores who have bruises on their legs or tattoos on their face. Emperor's Club VIP sold a different product than Dial-A-Slave. It was called "plumpkin" and involved sucking the client off while he took a shit. I understood how it could be so popular with politicians who shit on their constituencies.

I found myself back in the diner. We had all been given separate checks. I was vetting mine and didn't notice Sonya standing right in front of me. I knew I hadn't been daydreaming since no fantasy would have this kind of detail.

"I just wanted to explain why I had to break off our relationship."

We didn't have one, but I wasn't going to argue.

"It was because you got violent. I was afraid of what you might do to me. I had to walk home nude that night you threw me out of your apartment."

I was so excited I grabbed a glass of iced water and poured some drops over my head. I figured it was like taking extreme unction. I had to do something to purify myself before I strayed.

I suddenly regressed. I wasn't ready to see my need to devise increasingly violent sexual scenarios as a way to get stimulated as a sickness. I simply looked at myself as a horny or not so horny scumbag who liked walking on the wild side.

"We'll talk more," Sonya said.

There was a glint in her eye. I was frightened that my untruths were getting to her and that I was literally and metaphorically on the verge of pulling her chain again. I was like one of those hyenas you see on the nature documentaries looking up from the entrails they are eating with bloodstained lips.

I watched Sonya and Tiffany as they walked away, remembering Tiffany saying that even holding hands during the recitation of the Serenity Prayer at the end of a meeting could be a trigger. What would happen if I came up from behind and jammed my finger up her ass? I had once pulled a similar prank on my mother, who spanked me and told me to never do that again. Though it didn't stop me, I never forgot the admonition. Watching the two sluts walking into traffic, I realized I needed to start working the steps of the program if I were going to be a powerful example to other new Worms.

10

The Dream

I had a dream about Sonya that night. We were kissing passionately. I awoke with the feeling I hadn't experienced since high school, when I was in love with two bobbysoxers named Barbara and Ellen who wore tartans and Bass Weejuns. The outlines of their bras tantalized me through their preppy button-down collar shirts.

I'd reviled Sonya that infamous night, but this time woke up vacillating between the kind of disgust you feel at the sight of roadkill and guilt that now felt like love.

If it was love, I was cued into its medicinal effect by the hard-on I awakened with. I still didn't understand what was going on since the thought of what I'd done continued to repulse me.

A lot of people in the meetings give you their number. Sonya hadn't given me hers. I thought of calling Dial-a-Slave and asking them to leave a message, but I figured that was getting off on the wrong foot.

I reverted to magical thinking. If I were able to throw the little soap bar in my shower stall into the wastebasket by my toilet, I would run into her in Alphabet City. I walked carefully or more speedily down the stairs so that I would exit my building at the exact moment she was running by. And I kept thinking I was seeing her and having the same feeling of chasing after her while still wanting to run away.

I realized it was lucky my wishes weren't being fulfilled. The building itself would bring back the memories that wouldn't help either of us. I stood in front of the sign and descended into wormholes that landed me in worlds where our trajectories met and flourished. It was like going onto a porn site. In this case, for thrilling little moments in which my sadistic wishes were masked by romance.

In one of these descents, I saw her as she vanished down the steps in the Union Square station at rush hour. She was wearing that babushka again, and it partially covered her face. The crowd was like a riptide. The closer I tried to get, the more I was pushed away. Then, just as I caught up, the doors of the train closed behind her. She turned towards me with a look of longing.

Once I was back from the wormhole, in the safety of my familiar neighborhood, I realized I would just have to sit it out and pray. I would see Sonya at the meeting.

They say in the literature that "if you have been painstaking" in following the program "you will know how to deal with situations which baffle you." It had been decades since I'd asked a girl out on a date, but when I saw her the next day I simply walked up to her. She must have finally forgiven me or adjusted to the new me since she said "yes" when I asked if I could speak. However, she warned me she wasn't going to the Acropolis. Instead, she insisted that we meet right in the Downtown Cafe, just to keep things green.

When she sat down, she removed the babushka and shook her mane of black hair. Looking at someone eye to eye is a different kind of intimacy than watching them grovel at your feet. And for a moment I didn't know what I preferred. Though I'd awakened from my dream with feelings of longing, I wasn't even sure what I was experiencing. The desire for something I couldn't have was one thing, but seeing Sonya with her head covering off, I was caught up short and almost a little bored. Would I unwrap the package only to find myself replaying the same old tapes again, with me asking her to perform new tricks to ensure that I could still get it up?

"I had a dream…" I said.

"The reason I agreed to come out and see you," she cut in, "is to tell you how I feel. I've been with many men, but I never had a client like you, one who wanted to annihilate me in the way that you seemed intent on doing. I'm not blaming you. I hated myself and was looking for someone who would make me wish I were dead. You know, there's just as much a thrill in having your pride and spirit extinguished as in being the person who does it. Don't kid yourself. You weren't the only one who was getting off. I've had men do all kinds of things to me, but you're really gifted. You know how to skin a cat. When you ripped off all my clothes and left me whimpering on the cold floor of your doorway like a dog, it was the ultimate turn-on. You wouldn't fuck me, but it didn't matter."

She picked up her black kerchief and started to twirl it, like a cowboy does as he prepares a lasso in a rodeo. It was almost threatening. I pulled myself back in fear that she was going to whip me or wring my neck.

"Wait, the dream was not what you think." This time it was me interrupting to make a point. "We were talking and then we started to kiss. I've dreamt about plenty of girls but you're the first one I wanted to kiss. When I got up in the morning, I was missing you and looked for you everywhere."

"The program doesn't recommend any relationships during the first year," she said stiffly.

I could feel my body growing limp.

"Once you're settled with an identity and have found your place in the multiverse, then you may want to discuss it with a sponsor."

The gates of St. Peter were closing right in front of me. I was being forced to return to hell. But I had a hunch I could break her resolve.

However, then she would no longer be the girl in my dream that I wanted to kiss.

"Thanks so much for being so honest. I got a lot out of what you said. I have a sneaking and insidious disease that tells me I don't have disease. Sonya, it was great to hear you. It reminds me of the old 'feelings aren't facts.'"

I could see my words were having an effect on her. The puppet-like mimicking of what I'd heard at meetings was a spiritual aphrodisiac. It was as if I'd broken the ice. We were now prepared to sit back and remain content with nothing happening between us at all. Meetings gave you that kind of cozy feeling.

"I'm going to give you my meeting list," she said, sliding a thin worn-out, yellowing pamphlet, curled at the edges, towards me. "I've checked off and circled all the good ones. Except make sure you don't go to any of those marked 's' for sluts. Those are the women's meetings."

Even though the Wormhole Society was a relatively small organization only accessible to those who, like me, had been driven to find the portal to another life, there still were enough regular meetings to justify a written schedule.

"I couldn't after you have done all that work," I said, pushing the book away.

"It would really be meaningful for me to pass it on to you. I did the same with my ninety-day anniversary coin. I gave it away to another sick and suffering Worm."

I rubbed the book between my hands as if it were some sort of Christian relic like the Shroud of Turin, and I a pilgrim on his way to find the Holy Grail.

I'd never believed in anything or cared about anything. Wasn't this all supposed to be just a game, a way of passing the time until I could get it back up? Wasn't I like one of those drunks who detoxes to gets his system cleaned out so he can get hammered all over again? What was wrong with me? I was receiving the usual runaround and falling for it hook, line and sinker? For all I knew, Sonya was still turning tricks for Dial-a-Slave and just getting her jollies by trading places and getting me to submit to her will. I stared down at the pamphlet. I had to get to a meeting.

I needed Sonya's approval, but there was also a part of me that wanted to intone the inane little phrases and expressions. It was like omming in meditation. I said, "I'm Rusty and I'm a Worm" and everyone replied, "Hi Rusty." But when I looked down the list at the next meeting, I came across a little doodle of a cock. I was almost on the verge of holding it up in the air to point out the hypocrisy of everything when I stopped myself. First of all, it could have been her friend Tiffany who drew it. She had admitted to being perpetually horny. Secondly, I remembered the expression "you can look at your glass as being half full or half empty." It was progress not perfection. Even if the messenger had her problems and character defects, it didn't take away from the message.

11

Muriel

My upstairs neighbor Chip invited me to a rooftop Fourth of July party. When he saw me walk over to a girl who'd given me the eye, he whispered, "Because a girl is smiling at you doesn't mean she wants to have anal sex."

I'd seen him with lots of dates who weren't hookers. So I figured he knew something about relationships. And with these sage words of advice, I approached the young lady who appeared to be relationship material to the extent that she looked well-adjusted and self-confident—two things I was not.

I had an immediate fantasy about hooking up with someone who would show me the ropes, in terms of what it meant to be "normal."

Sensing I was approaching, she coyly turned away.

"Wait a minute," Chip cautioned. "Let her come to you."

When she turned in my direction, I said, "I didn't get your name."

"Muriel."

Without needing to go to the sandwich board outside the Downtown Cafe, I entered an alternate universe where females possessed names like Muriel, Sybil, Ethel, Olive, Midge, Beverly and Betty.

"Like the character played by Delphine Seyrig in the Resnais film," she added.

I was a little put off by the namedropping, but I was also in a mood where I was attracted to practically any form of knowledge.

I saw us in our own Grant Wood American Gothic, sitting in our rockers on the porch of some swingers club where the younger crowd were raving inside, while we were exiled to the porch with ball gags in our mouths.

What do people who have practiced S&M and bondage on a massive scale, look like when they get older?

"What do you do?" she reluctantly asked.

"I teach English as a second language, but I'm taking a little hiatus."

"I like that. It's honest work. Better than my former husband who fucked everything in sight."

"You look like an artist."

"Close, I work at Pearl Paint, the art supply store on Canal Street."

I conjured up my sandwich board and escaped into a wormhole in which Muriel was an exotic French actress of the '60s, then a submissive in a Cicero, Illinois crack house. People never realize it, but these little expeditions can occur instantaneously since you're only being transmitted from the might-have-been to the have-yet-to-be.

I made one of these little trips while Muriel was yawning. I could see she hadn't had her tonsils out yet. I am still triggered by a woman opening her mouth to talk or just to swallow something. I look at it as an invitation to oral sex. I flew into the same place in the fifteenth century, where I accidentally came upon Saint Teresa's transverberation, her marriage with God, during a point in the conversation when Muriel grabbed a handful of dried Planter's Peanuts and shoved them into her mouth.

The fireworks started in a succession of booms that were followed by dramatic fountains of colored light. But neither of us got up to join the others, who ascended to the roof. We found ourselves alone in my friend's living room.

Muriel was now talking rather animatedly about her former husband, who was a personal trainer.

"You can't imagine. You think you know someone, and they've been lying. You know, those sinkholes into which people disappear."

Though I nodded as if I understood, it was as if she were speaking another tongue. When I put my arm around her shoulder, she pulled it off, taking me by the hand and leading me into the small adjacent bedroom. She pulled a cord that closed the slats of the venetian blinds.

"Let's make out," she said.

I had the distinct memory of a sex-ed teacher in high school saying how important one's first sexual experience was. The very *first* sex act I'd experienced was with an anonymous mouth on the other side of our local glory hole establishment, in the cinder block storage bunker, behind a Hess station.

As another set of explosions occurred in the distance, the night sky was lit up with a huge sparkling efflorescence of color.

She turned off the light. I couldn't see her. Our heads butted into each other. She let out a cry just as another explosion went off and flipped the light back on, just as I was thinking that that the kissing and cracking of fireworks were the perfect way to celebrate the Fourth.

Her eyes were tearing, in the way they do when someone punches you in the nose. I couldn't believe that my first attempt at kissing would result in a rhinoplasty.

It wasn't a matter of whether we were good or bad for each other, as much as we'd found each other.

We would have looked like the perfect romantic couple when we met for a candlelit dinner at Lucien, the local French place on First Avenue for our first real date several days later—if it weren't for the black rings under her eyes from the injury and the golf ball protruding from my forehead.

I ordered the coq au vin, pronouncing it like "cock."

"It's coq like Coke," Muriel corrected cheerily, as our ladyboy server's lips began to tremble. I was thinking she might be the one since she was tolerant of my mispronunciation.

"I'll have Tim's balls," I thought she said, realizing when I looked down at the menu that she was ordering something called "timbale."

"So here we are." Though she was plainly happy to see me, she was obviously exasperated. Seeing the swelling on my forehead only accentuated the memory of our little comeuppance.

You don't usually visualize a romantic couple looking like train wrecks, after a disaster.

I thought she was about to laugh, but it turned out to be an asthma attack.

"Maybe I should have had the cock," Muriel said, sniffing her inhaler and seeming to validate me by choosing the wrong word.

I took the cue and reached across the table for her hand. I started to play with her fingers. The problem was that, having no experience with romantic candlelit dinners, I didn't know how to stop. When the food came, she couldn't pick up her utensils. Everything was getting cold since we were both afraid to break the mood by disengaging.

Finally, when she slithered her now sweaty palm from mine, I made my big play, grabbing her to me. My grand gesture caused Muriel's wine glass to spill all over the table.

The manager came over with a fresh cloth.

Lucien was the kind of place you went for a quiet civilized dinner. We stood there awkwardly as the rest of the diners glanced furtively at the beaten-up looking couple who were disrupting their meals.

We tried to turn it all into humor. I joked about "eating my cock."

She arched her eyebrows seductively, asking if I wanted to taste her sole.

As we stared at each other over the candlelit lantern that been placed before us after the last accident, I reached into my wallet, took out a $50 bill and pushed it across the table.

"I'd feel much better if you took this."

"Why?"

"Services to be rendered."

"Huh?" she said with a tone of instant indignation

"Just kidding." I said, trying to salvage the evening.

Muriel picked her purse up from the floor, snapped it shut, grabbed her coat from the back of her chair and ran out of the restaurant.

"It was just a joke," I cried out.

I caught up to her on the street a block away, but she refused to stop when I called her name. She brushed me off as I attempted to hold her arm. I could see she was crying and her mascara had smeared—which got me hard.

"My husband liked to play these kinds of games, so I know what you're doing."

Muriel was obviously not going to be hurt again. The minute she got wind of the thoughts going through my head, she would have nothing to do with me. Taking a few quick dips into the wormhole, I was hard put to find any versions of Muriel who would either.

I felt so despondent, I started to walk towards the Bang Bang Club, thinking I deserved some kind of reward for all my travails.

I had rushed in headfirst with Muriel and ended up with some lacerations. This was an example of a "geographic," one of the common avoidance mechanisms talked about at meetings, if there ever was one. It was one thing to go after a new identity and another to just run away.

I would tie one on, then hit a meeting the next day. Who knew? Maybe I'd get lucky. Could Sonya be turning tricks to finance her recovery?

12

Submission

Even though my relationship with Muriel never really began, I went through a period of mourning after our breakup. I liked her. I had really tried to behave myself. I felt she was overreacting to my trying to pay her for sex. After all, I had previously paid everyone else for it. I looked at the incident as a misunderstanding we could have gotten over if she had given me a chance to explain my behavior in the context of my life.

One afternoon after cruising along Canal and only exchanging eye contact with the dead fish lying on ice in the open-air Chinese markets, I walked over to Pearl Paint with its distinctive red and white checkered awning. Through the window, I could see her attending to a Chinese artist with long white hair that ran down to his shoulders.

I walked in and tried to get her attention. She pretended she didn't know me.

"But you were my lady girl," I muttered with tears in my eyes. "I love you…"

"Sorry, he's next," she said turning to another customer.

I couldn't get Muriel out of my mind. I was so depressed, I foolishly stopped going to meetings. I'd made Muriel into a drug. Now I needed help with the withdrawal.

I couldn't stand the thought of all the bright faces attesting to the happiness they had found in the multiverse. I didn't think I would ever be one of them. Though I still looked at Sonya like the girls in peep show booths to whom my dirty talk was a form of confession, I couldn't bear to hear any more of her pious declarations about the program.

If nothing mattered, then why waste energy traveling back and forth in time, in search of a personality I would ultimately be incompatible with? Up until then I still had the desire to humiliate those I had sex with, even if it was no longer arousing me—if for no other reason than not knowing anything different. It wasn't as if I'd gone through a sea change and become a better person. I knew I hadn't learned anything. I secretly was just looking to get myself back to the point where I could start my old life up again. But it was also true that there were times when I was cruising through space that I felt like one of those effervescent tablets, an Alka-Seltzer that fizzes when dissolved in a glass of water. There was no doubt that, in the solitary moments when I stood before the sandwich board outside The Downtown Cafe, changes were taking place despite all my stubborn efforts to resist them— changes that I wasn't even sure I wanted to occur.

One hot weekend I fell asleep on the A. I was headed for a public swimming pool in Woodhaven and ended up at Beach 67 Street in the Rockaways. I watched the rolling surf in the hope that I would find some answers. Staring out at the vastness of the ocean provided solace, but by the end of a day I only ended up lonely and sunburned.

Walking along the deserted stretch of Surfer's Beach (where swimming wasn't permitted), I came across a bikini-clad girl lying on her back rocking her spread legs suggestively. Her eyes were covered by aviator sunglasses. The straps of her top were undone and the suntan lotion she was applying to her arms glistened in the heat.

She was literally sizzling.

I dropped a $20 bill on her breast, making it look like an accident. But my shady come-on produced a world-weary look. She raised her arm with the bill between her fingers, as if to say, "Been there, done that."

I was heartened when I saw that she'd been reading *Slave*, the erotic novel that was the centerpiece of the Showtime series *Submission*. I'd thought the book was literally a fiction, an ornament created for the series. I was excited to see it was real. The book had obviously been read and reread. The corners of the pages were curling.

"I'm suffering from macular degeneration," I lied. "It would be a great solace if you could read to me from that lovely book."

"I had a hunch you couldn't see," she said, picking the $20 bill off the sand. "You can always tell a book by its cover."

She tied her hair into a ponytail to keep it out of her eyes and began reading with me standing right over her.

I was totally naked. He spread-eagled me, shackling my arms and legs to the four-poster... She stopped, just before the main character Ashley is gagged and blindfolded.

I dropped my wallet in the sand, fumbling nervously to find another bill. In the distance I could see a gray-shingled bungalow with broken and boarded up windows. It would be a cinch to break into. A squatter's paradise, it would be the perfect place for an interlude of rough sex.

She picked up her towel and imperiously blurted out "don't press" when I asked if she'd let me take a yank on her ponytail, just one time.

I felt sorry for myself. Why me? I would have gladly offered her more money to talk dirty while waves broke in the distance. I would have accompanied her over the threshold of the public bathroom marked "Men." Or, if she were all talked out, I could have put a rubber Spalding in her mouth. I would have offered to handcuff her, though it would have ended up being just an empty promise since there were no nearby branches of the Pleasure Chest, my favorite sex shop.

The skies had been otherwise blue and clear, but I quickly noticed a shift in the upper atmosphere. Now there were dark threatening clouds. They looked like they were about to burst. Everything was happening quickly. Suddenly, with a crack of thunder and a flash in the distance, it was pouring.

People ran for cover. As I headed for the elevated changing rooms, I was stunned by a shock that rumbled through my body and then sent me flying onto the sand.

Had I actually been hit by lightning? It's lucky I was still on the beach where the ground was soft. Who knew what would have happened if I'd been thrown to the sidewalk? It obviously wasn't a big strike since I had survived, and with only a few burn marks, little punctures of the skin surrounded by bruises on my legs and arms. The effect reminded me a little of the shock I'd felt when I stuck my finger in a socket as a kid.

Saul of Tarsus had been blinded by a light from above on the road to Damascus. I too had been struck, though I had yet to have any revelation. I couldn't stop thinking about the busty bitch, her body slathered in oil, even as my body shook. I secretly hoped she had at least gotten a little fried by the electricity in the air. I imagined her vibrating in a good way as the shock ran through her.

I realized I'd gotten off easy, but rather than being thankful I hoped the electricity would rejuvenate my own declining sexual powers. Electroshock was used on inmates of insane asylums. Maybe it could work as an aphrodisiac. I was perfectly willing to wet my fingers and stick them in a socket if that got me hard.

Behind the stalls of the toilets, I could hear male voices, as they changed out of their wet clothes.

"My nuts are covered with sand."

"Did you see the wet T-shirt contest?"

"Did you see the tits on that bitch?"

"Yeah, her nipples stood at attention like guards at Buckingham Palace."

"*Their* nipples. They insist on being called they," I interjected. What better place to apply my Wormhole Society experience!

I hated the doggerel written on the walls of stalls, nonsense rhymes that always ended with the offer of free blowjobs. However, I picked up my cell phone and responded to one of the numbers, following a series of prompts on the voice message, which offered a choice of "immediate" or "delayed gratification" or the option to "speak to a representative."

At this point, considering the downpour, I knew that traveling millions of light years would get me home faster than public transit—though, when you went into a wormhole, you of course always ran the risk of becoming waylaid in another life.

I closed my eyes and visualized the sandwich board of The Downtown Cafe, feeling like that last bit of dirty water letting out a gurgling sound as it swirls down the drain. This time I didn't go anywhere. I ended up back in the men's changing room. When I came to, I was sitting on the same wooden bench.

I hadn't gone anywhere.

I panicked, thinking I'd lost my powers.

The rain had stopped. The sunlight was almost blinding, but I could see that there was something about the ocean and the shoreline that was totally different from what I had experienced earlier in the day.

I noticed several women walking by in 1920s-style swimming costumes. I had begun my journey home by falling into a chink in time, but what had made me choose this particular era? Was it the illusion that life was simpler and less filled with temptations when the female body was less exposed? Besides not knowing what I really wanted, I obviously still didn't have the slightest idea of how to effectively navigate a wormhole.

I called the sandwich board up again and this time found myself planted right in front of my building. I looked at my watch, saw that it was 5:30 p.m. on July 21. I realized I had my whole life back—at least the life I'd always lived, in the dimension I'd been born into. Nothing had changed, but I'd gotten home a lot faster than I would have on the A.

13

Wormholing

I had to be careful. I could inadvertently be wafted into a wormhole, whenever the sandwich board came into my mind.

I found myself wandering in a grove. The path was what I was looking for since the topiaries were now crushing in on me, creating a literal coffin of shrubbery. The only thing I'd ever seen like it was the thick pine forests of Northern Maine which were as difficult to permeate as they were to escape from. The bush, the shrubbery, "the thing," whatever it might be called, was now encroaching on me. The nettles of the branches were starting to sting. Was I dreaming or really in danger of being suffocated?

I panicked and tried to push away the foliage, but the more I exhausted myself using brute force, the more entangled I became. Certain kinds of knots grow tighter the more you try to free yourself from them. In my desperation I used my fist as a kind of drill, hoping that if I calmed my anxiety enough to burrow a small hole, I would eventually be able to make it large enough to crawl through.

I might as well have been Harold Lloyd hanging from the hands of a clock in the famous silent film *Safety Last*. It would have been one thing if I'd left my apartment, gone to the Downtown Cafe and stared at the sandwich board or even imaged it in my mind, but my current descent into the wormhole had happened all by itself, with no warning.

The floor had given way under me. I had read about a poor guy in Florida who was buried alive when he fell into the sinkhole beneath his bed. Days passed before they could dig out his corpse.

Were wormholes like steroids that produced unwanted side effects after prolonged use?

I desperately tried to recall the sandwich board as I had many times in the past, but it wasn't working. Instead of finding a street or signpost as I walked further, the grove seemed to swallow me up until I was imprisoned by the menacing animal-shaped topiaries.

"Halfway along our life's path…" I remembered the first words of Dante's *Inferno*, for which I demonstrated an uncanny understanding, considering my otherwise lackluster academic performance. My freshman English teacher wanted to know how I gained so much knowledge about the Ninth Circle of Hell. I told her it was all very familiar if you hang out in certain parts of town—something she had found funny, but I knew was true.

She covered herself and abruptly ended our discussion when she noticed that I was staring down her blouse.

I remembered *The Great Escape*, the movie about the POWs who free themselves from a Nazi prison camp by digging a tunnel. Only now every time I made a little progress, my exit seemed to fill up with even more determined branches and roots that reprimanded my own desire to live, filling up the space with an intensity that was greater than my ability to ply their formations apart.

I gasped for air. I awakened in a sweat, the shortage of breath accounted for simply by the fact that I was lying face down on my pillow. I often slept on my stomach. It wasn't unusual that, along with grinding my teeth, I would cut off my air by pulling myself tightly down when I was either having a wet dream or trying to subdue an intruder in my sleep.

I began to hyperventilate and was sure I was going to faint as the gnashing teeth of a wild boar came at me.

"God!" I cried.

I swooped back to the familiar church basement. The others at the meeting started to shake me. Then there was a clap and then a thunderous round of applause. The whole group was beaming at me.

"I'm Rusty and I'm a grateful recovering member of this program."

The rest of the room, including Sonya and Tiffany who were standing together, replied "Hi Rusty."

I might have been speaking in tongues or squeaky clean from a ritual bath, but I secretly knew that I was still a danger to society.

My first qualification in the WS had by all accounts been a success. Of course, everyone was greeted with superlatives. I'd never heard anything but praise for even the most hopeless cases.

I climbed into a wormhole right after hanging out with the others in front of the church. I entered a parallel universe that put me in the middle of a session Cliff and I would have in a few weeks. I have heard that it's OK when the therapist is one step ahead of the patient. Due to the different time zones, the problem with wormholing and therapy was that you sometimes ended up hearing things that you were ready for.

Cliff couldn't stop laughing when I told him all about the topiaries that were coming for me. He was apparently a little weirder than I thought. Most people don't crack up when you describe how you were suffocating.

I think he could tell from the expression on my face that something was wrong because he immediately tried to cover his tracks.

"It's just so incredibly real. I shouldn't say this since it may excite you, but I had a similar situation occur just when I was developing what's the equivalent of mental telepathy in the universe of wormholes. I love women with big asses, but I had this big hot momma sitting on my face and I couldn't breathe."

I thanked Cliff, set up our next appointment that was over a month away (in real time or at least the time from which I'd originally come) and bee-lined back to my present existence.

14

Lucy

I was at the dawn of recorded time, which was more than I had bargained for. It all looked like an episode from *The Flintstones*. I could see that the caveman, emerging from his thatched hut with his wife and bone in tow, was upset by something. He was gesturing towards his crotch and throwing his hands up to the heavens. Could the advent of consciousness have coincided with man's first failure to get it up?

But this was only the starting point. When you are wormholing, there are lots of choices. It's like looking through the Sears catalogue. You can go backwards or forwards or just sideways, playing with little variations that may be a millisecond apart. The dimensions are like filo dough with infinite subtle variations between the layers.

The couple I spotted had the features of Neanderthals.

There were also some Cro-Magnon chicks. I called out "yo"— a greeting universally acknowledged by man and beast throughout time—just to be friendly. I took off, homing in on an early ancestor of man, *Homo erectus*, who lived 1.9 million years ago.

I hoped that belonging to a species with a name like that would solve my problems. I'd read several articles online about Harry Reems and

John Holmes, porn stars known for their staying power, having DNA similar to apes.

However, as I came closer to my goal, I experienced a sense of déjà vu, spotting the reflection of an unshaven creature covered only by an animal skin in a local watering hole. It wasn't long before I realized he was a primitive version of myself, another neurotic guy, my doppelganger from the Pleistocene era, who also happened to be upset with his sex life.

When you journey to one of these parallel universes, you're instantaneously equipped with a whole getup and backstory. I was plainly one of them and spoke the lingo. But I could tell right away by the body language of the other "villagers" that I wasn't a particularly respected member of the tribe. I had brought my reputation for being a sleazeball with me into the multiverse with my wide-eyed leering and state of constant amazement. While most of the women didn't have any choice in the matter, I could see they were avoiding making eye contact with me. They plainly weren't happy with the notion they might be offered up by their families for whatever dowry I could command.

I was getting the cold shoulder even though, if correct, I had been the first example of Stone Age man to create fire (millennia earlier) and then build a hot tub. Along with the backstory, I had a whole future history, but there were the equivalent of traffic rules when you travelled through wormholes. Your access to your future (or past) was quarantined. It was essentially impossible to avail yourself of it—though you could do all the daydreaming you wanted about sizzling steaks or houses warmed by solar panels.

Even though it was a tribal society, many of us mated freely. In fact, the caveman experience was as close as I would get to the joys of being an animal. Monogamy may have been ages away, but we were slowly evolving from the kind of animal sex where you mounted the nearest creature in the mosh pit, to the beginnings of having likes and dislikes. Despite my bad rep, I still had my pick when it came to one-night stands. A lot of these chicks were on the verge of having their consciousness created and even raised but, happily, hadn't gotten there yet.

Having all these babes I could routinely throw to the ground and fuck at will would have been a great idea, if I got an erection. Compensating for my performance anxiety had become the bane of my existence. But before packing it in, I decided I at least had to give time travel through parallel universes a more thorough try. After all, there were an infinite number of coordinates; there had to be some time and place in which I could find the right recipe. Somewhere there was a form of myself where I'd be able to succeed—hopefully without the need for the degradation and humiliation which were no longer helping me to get my rocks off anyway.

Sure, Caligula's Rome was about as permissive as you get, but I was trying to stay away from the Caracalla baths because of all the debauchery. Been there, done that. Seeing I was in my back-to-nature phase, I decided to continue going backwards rather than forward. So, shooting further down the wormhole I'd been traveling in, I journeyed back 3.2 million years and found Lucy, an example of a species called *Australopithecus afarensis* who made headlines when she was discovered in an Ethiopian village in 1974.

Traveling three million years into the past is a little different from the hop, skip and jump that had got me in with a bunch of erect homo something or others, who only made me feel inferior. But if you picked the right wormhole, you were going to end up travelling way past the speed of light in terms of the amount of space/time that's transpired. So that wasn't the problem. It's just that returning to the era when toolmaking first came into fashion can result in culture shock—particularly when it comes to creature comforts and amenities.

I had seen naked photos of Lucy's skeletal remains. Necrophilia isn't my bag, but from the paleontological point of view, she was really a hot item. I was awakening from a deep sleep the first time I laid eyes on her (the use of "them" for "her" didn't come about until our present Cenozoic era). I was lying in a grove surrounded by huge banyan trees on which monkeys swung from vines.

I had no idea I would see "Lucy" on my first day. It would have been something akin to spotting a famous actress like Jodie Foster in the East Village. But the moment I laid eyes on Lucy squatting to take a dump in the brush, there was no mistaking her. She stood out among a crowd of other Australopithecus females who were obviously taking a break at the Pliocene equivalent of the roadside women's room that can be found on I-95.

The others were equally cute in the way they squatted and deftly tossed their leaves away after wiping themselves. But Lucy had a certain bowlegged swagger and pride in her pile that made her stand out from the others, who didn't seem as lit up about having successfully moved their bowels. You could see it in the structure of her high aristocratic cheekbones, and from the long uninterrupted brow I had previously noted in computer simulations of her face.

Now that I was in a position to confront the real McCoy, I cried out the equivalent of "wow"—*abbey, abbey, abbey*—when I saw her nude form emerging from the brush. I also figured I would use some of the advantage of my superior knowledge of yoga to get her attention by doing a downward dog. Only three feet tall, she was smaller than what we call petite. If I could get it up, I was going to be too big for her (I'd forgotten my Astroglide when I began my journey into the past). But then when our eyes met, I saw right away that I was only a little bit taller in my Australopithecus form and realized there would be no problem.

The fact that we were both hirsute only served to grease our wheels. I have always liked the natural look anyway. My heart pounded when I realized Lucy was a good three million years away from Brazilian waxing.

Bay, bay, bay, Lucy called out. This translates roughly to "You ain't half bad yourself." *Australopithecus afarensis* chicks are not coy like your average *Homo erectus*. They quickly lay their cards on the table, which, in Lucy's case, took the form of her grabbing a handful of berries and rubbing them across their face. She seemed to think that was funny though I was pretty turned on, finding myself accessing some old tapes that still ran through my head. I figured my fantasy-fueled passion was a harmless lie, which would rid me of any residual performance anxiety and allow me to successfully perform the deed. Neither of us would be worse for the wear. No sense in journeying over epochs of human evolution only to find a wilted carrot between my legs. The look on a woman or for that matter ladyboy's face was the same whether you were in 2025 or 2, 997,985 BC. I couldn't bear to hear Lucy saying, *Na, na, na*, which means "What's wrong?"

However, I didn't even have time to feel any guilt about my thoughts. Before I knew it, she threw me to the ground and mounted me. She was nothing like the kind of twenty-first century women who complain you weren't paying attention to their needs when you thoughtlessly pummeled them with your dick. No sooner had we done it than we were wrestling in the mud as I pushed away male interlopers horning in on the action.

It turns out that the closer you get to the Big Bang, the hotter the passions unleashed. After we were done and I was totally spent, she hoisted me over her shoulder and carried me to the top of her favorite tree.

I was soon awakened from the post-coital spooning position in which we dozed by a fresh throbbing in my crotch, heightened by the thought of adding a famous paleontological specimen as a notch on my belt. I could see that even though Lucy was not the kind of chick you'd pick from central casting to play the lead in *The Story of O*, there was nevertheless something very wanton about the way she went after what she wanted. I couldn't help regarding it as an invitation when she reached behind herself, pulled a banana off a tree and waved it at me. Then as Lucy entered an even more ecstatic state, what the tantric sex people back in the future describe as an out-of-body experience, she called out *Bluh, bluh, bluh*, which because I was now one of them and participated in the equivalent of Google translator, I knew meant "Fuck me in the ass." Anything went. I found myself sucking her teat which had a smell I'd never experienced before, something between a vacuum cleaner bag and the kind of solvent that's used to stain wood.

Finally, after my deprived childhood, I was getting the maternal love I never had, to the accompaniment of a new medley of olfactory sensations. I was not only satiated but cared for and loved almost from the beginning. I was falling head over heels for her. I not only had no desire to get away from her, as I did most women who I had sullied, I wanted to stay and found myself following her around as the sun set. I faced a choice of leaving or hanging out with her for the night.

I might have died and gone to heaven but, nevertheless, I remembered the suggestion made at the Wormhole Society meetings about not getting into new relationships in the first year. I might know what I want, but did I know what I needed?

Being prehensile creatures, walking on our own two feet, it was easy to show Lucy my tools. *Homo erectus* indeed! I smiled to myself as I stared up at the smog-free skies of the primeval rainforest. Human consciousness was developing right before my eyes, as I lay on my back drinking milk from a coconut with one hand and stroking my hard cock with the other.

I knew that trying to convince Lucy she was going to become a figure of world historical importance, a celebrity in the world of paleontology, was going to be taken as a rather obvious attempt at flattery. The way the idea of celebrity was communicated in Australopithecanese was for me to point at Lucy and jump up and down like a hyena.

Her dwelling, literally the place we first hung out as we dangled from overhanging branches, was simply a mud slab. It reminded me of my mother's exclamation about my room when I was a kid: "It looks like a pigsty." But I remember the day we found the "flat" where we would cohabitate. Being out in the open on gorgeous virgin land, our residence was a lot nicer than any of the apartments you will find on Craigslist. Naturally, there were no broker's fees involved. Still, I could see Lucy's long brow furrowing as she pondered if this was the spot where we would nest.

These early hunter-gatherers had not yet developed to the point where they learned to share their feelings, as we would eventually do in our Wormhole meetings. I tried to conceive of Lucy as someone I could learn from, instead of being just another chick I could test my masculinity on. After all, she was a real survivor (from a skeletal point of view). So, at the very least I was going to pick up something about orthopedics. Would I rather have a boner or figure out how to avoid arthritis from someone who had amazing bones?

Though Lucy could be moody and obsessed with nuts, she wasn't the kind of neurotic you were likely to meet on the Lower East Side. While I was going back and forth in my head, her life was simple and straightforward. She wasn't thinking in terms of relationships or what the future held.

If you interrupted her while she was squatting to crack an acorn, she might even purposefully stomp on your foot in annoyance. Even for a prime example of *Australopithecus afarensis*, she was a piece of work. When she was having her period, which was readily visible, you had to watch out for her murderous rage. On more than one occasion I ended up limping away, after she exploded and threw her nuts at me, but that was the extent of it.

I had no idea what I was getting into. When I least expected it, Lucy's hormones would kick in and she was like a dog in estrus. She would chase me all over the place. I delighted in playing hard to get as I ducked in and out of the bush, which was our backyard, until she gave up the nuts and wrestled me to the ground.

Neither Lucy nor I had had much experience standing on our own two feet, since it had only been a couple of hundred thousand years since our species had developed. And when it came to using my tool there was a steep learning curve. For instance, after our first tumble in the hay I asked, *Yak abu, abu*, which means "How was I?" Even though it was natural for a wormhole traveler to speak the local lingo, it was odd to hear these strange sounds emanate from my mouth.

She responded, *Shabu, shabu*, which simply means "fine"—really not the response you are looking for. I thought she might stick her ass up in the air and scream out *Yak, yak, yak*, which means "Do it again"—obviously the kind of compliment I am bucking for. But no cigar! Lucy was perfectly capable of being coy, which meant not answering when I sought validation. She had a dry wit and could also be a tart conversationalist with her *Bim, bim, bim*, which means "Sure, sure." She spiked her repartee with little ball-busting gibes that always kept me on my hairy toes.

Even though she was only a primitive ancestor, in some ways she had traits that were remarkably like those of Muriel. She had a hands-on pragmatic side that was almost demanding. Back in those days there was little for couples to do beyond making a fire—the equivalent of one of those state-of-the art entertainment centers folks have in their homes. I knew it was time to rub my sticks together when she pushed her chin into her chest and intoned, *Hiyah, hiyah*. The burst of fire when the spark hit the sticks and leaves we had gathered was always a big thrill for which we expressed our awe by intoning yak. And when I suggested hunting and gathering, which was done more in signs than sounds, she looked at me skeptically as if to ask, "What are we going to do for the rest of the night?" Then she answered her own question by mimicking the thrusting movements a male of any species makes when they're about to come.

Just the way a picture speaks a thousand words, her matter-of-fact facial expressions told the whole story. Screwing was everything. When that was over there was nothing else to do but gaze at the wonder of fire, in the same way we marvel at high-speed internet connections.

I liked Lucy more than I did Muriel and started thinking about making a life with her on the veldt. There was no way of expressing the idea of living together, but we both found ourselves pointing to the ground beneath our feet. This was how the adult Australopithecus demonstrated commitment. Little piles of fruits and berries were the signs of our domesticity. When Lucy wasn't aping my behavior—like the way she blew fart sounds between her lips when I couldn't seem to control my need to lay really smelly ones—she was busily climbing every tree in sight. For a woman she was really strong.

I could hardly catch her as she deftly made her way up a new trunk, whistling for me to follow. I have always had this problem of trying to keep up with the Joneses. I got myself into a few hairy situations in which she had to swing down to pull me up to the next branch. At first, I was staying in back so I could look up her hole. However, it soon became apparent I couldn't reciprocate by putting myself in a position where she was looking up my wazoo—if I wanted to. I was simply out of my league when it came to these kinds of ascents.

That was one of the nice things about being one of the later Neanderthals. Girls weren't uptight and shame had yet to be invented since it would be hundreds of millions of years before Adam and Eve had their fall. In fact, Lucy seemed to enjoy flashing me and would cry out, *Boo hoo, boo hoo,* when she caught me staring at her snatch. This reminded me of a girl named Francesca, a redhead in my third-grade class who got in trouble for pulling her dress up in the schoolyard.

I didn't have the same problems with Lucy that I had with Muriel when it came to turning her into a whore. The Australopithecus existed in what this dude Lewis Hyde, on a TED Talk, termed a "gift economy"—in which there is no such thing as paying for sex or anything else for that matter. You simply bartered. I gave Lucy a coconut. If she liked the milk, she let me lick her tits. It was in this uncomplicated and stress-free atmosphere that for the first time I learned what lovemaking was all about.

One of the first times we went at it, she was crawling along the ground on all fours when I grabbed her from behind. There wasn't a hint of submission in the position. The muscles inside her vagina were so strong I couldn't have pulled out if I wanted to. It was like being sucked into a lubricious vise that squeezed the juice out of my prick as if the shaft were a citrus fruit. When we were done, we both lay exhausted on the ground, licking each other and eating the grass.

The Australopithecus were believers in free love, but they didn't really know it since they still had the kinds of bicameral minds that didn't lead to what we experience as self-reflexive thought. I could never say something to Lucy like "What are you thinking about?" Or if I wasn't getting it up, she would not have said to me I was thinking too much. Instead, she might knit her thick wizened eyebrows together before uttering *Yx, yx, yx,* which freely translated means "Fuck you." A look of what I would call skepticism crossed her hairy face with its heavy jaw. Afterwards, she'd scamper off to find another partner. Lucy wouldn't have experienced guilt about cheating on me anymore than I was supposed to be possessive, or vice versa.

The ancestors of man, like Lucy, were incapable of realizing they were thinking, but it wasn't as if things didn't occur to them. For instance, one of the delicacies we dined upon as a kind of pre-dinner hors d'oeuvre were insects. I'd wager that Lucy had a better knowledge of what was flying over the top of a pond than most experienced fly fisherman. This was the kind of thought she specialized in. Even though she may have been unaware she was thinking it, she would point to a tiny bug about to prey upon some creature lower down on the food chain like a slow-moving beetle hanging out on a floating lily. She would put a finger to her lips to show me how one approaches a situation like this without making a sound. She loved worms (not the kind who attended meetings) and seemed to intuitively know what rocks they crawled under. She was the mentor and I the student when it came to foraging expeditions.

The kind of thinking that we Australopithecus did demonstrate, which was mostly related to survival and procreation, probably explains why I felt liberated from my obsessions. Civilization had not evolved to the point where there were fetishes. As attracted to Lucy as I was within the confines of the Pliocene era, I couldn't have imagined her in a lacy black bra and garter belt. It was hard to conceive of her putting stockings on those hairy legs. She hadn't learned about role-playing either. Since I was another member of the species I was attracted to her smell, which was similar to that of a sweaty dog, but Lucy wasn't the kind of gal who would perform slave tricks at the Bang Bang Club. I didn't see her as Miss Lucy, a dominatrix waving a cat o' nine tails in her hand—though who knows if the branch she was always holding couldn't be used as a switch. Back home in Manhattan sex was complicated. However, language was never a problem. Here, though, the sex was simple. Lucy and I were never at a loss for words—since we depended on sounds. I had the same desire to ask how I was in comparison to other males, but no way to express it.

The most important part of my whole adventure was that as an *Australopithecus afarensis*, I wasn't even aware I was having sex when I was having it—which is most likely one of the reasons I was usually able to get it up. I simply wasn't overthinking everything like I did when I was living in a world of *Homo sapien* fantasy.

Our life was so much about fruits and vegetables I contemplated opening up a twenty-four-hour Korean market. Even though there was no money, I experienced a prosperity that made me feel I'd arrived.

No doubt this parallel universe was the right place for me. These hunters and gatherers bartered seeds and grapes for carcasses. Imagining myself as the first capitalist in the history of the world, I was freely able to indulge my animal appetites, yet with none of the crazy stuff that now filled me with guilt and shame. There had been no pharaoh or Civil War. Lucy didn't even know what slavery was. Telling her to get down on all fours, to ferret through some shrubs, was not very much of a demotion since being an early hominid, she was still a little shaky on two feet.

I would simply utter *Blix, booha, booha*. She'd respond happily with a *Brrrm, boohoo, brrrrr*. We would have been on the same page even if we hadn't said anything. There were times, in fact, when the two of us scavenging for insects or dead birds looked like denizens of the old Hellfire Club, which had once been one of the most notorious S&M venues in the meatpacking district—especially on nights when they conducted the slave auction.

However, there was a huge difference between hopping around on all fours to hunt for tender beetles, crunchy water bugs or sweet tasting ants and crawling on all fours because someone was trying to convince you that you were a lower form of life.

I had to decide whether I wanted to give up my sadistic fantasies for a world where I'd see my partner merrily running through the brush to catch a snake. Even though I liked to read, I had never been a real intellectual. The fact that Lucy and I didn't discuss books or any of the major issues of the day was no loss. *Ek, ek, ek* and *Bdp, bdp, bdp* made a lot more sense to me then heated discussions about the Middle East situation, the minimum wage or whether existence preceded essence. Due to this lack of consciousness, neither Lucy nor any of her friends ever mused about life, death or how the world came into being. While we did plenty of innocent gangbanging with some willing friends, I was the only one capable of thinking about the Big Bang (which I once tried to demonstrate to Lucy by thrusting particularly vigorously when I was about to come).

You'd think some of my recondite knowledge would have leaked out, but that wasn't the way this whole parallel universe thing worked. In fact, a Berlin Wall stood between your two selves. There was no danger of the butterfly effect, in which the past or future are modified due to time travel.

Sometimes I felt very alone and misunderstood because of this. No matter how hard I tried to water things down, it was virtually impossible to get my knowledge across to Lucy. I had this whole memory bank, but none of it came out when I was chatting gaily with her in our native tongue about the *blx, blx, blx* or the *robey, robey*.

To Lucy, I was just another Australopithecus male. This was the key to these kinds of parallel universes. There was no substance to the old fear that someone like me could go into the past and accidentally change the future. It didn't happen because when I descended into a wormhole, I became part of the time I visited. Similarly, any fears I had that people back in the present might have missed me and especially that I might have been evicted from my rent stabilized apartment were also dispelled, as my departure no more shook up the present than it did the future or past.

I started to have a life in the Pliocene era until one night while Lucy slept I woke up in a panic. If I lost my powers, I would be stuck millions of years in the past. Further, even if I made it back to the present, I was scared I would look like the diminutive hairy *Australopithecus afarensis* I'd become.

So, I brought up my favorite sandwich board, wormholed my way back and landed right where I'd left off, making sure that Nelsa made my burrito the way I liked it with onions and extra avocado.

For a moment I didn't know where I was. All the traffic and taxis honking were a huge contrast to the teeming hum of nature. Everything seemed strange. I felt like I'd been away for ages—which in this case I really had. *Slrrp, slrrp, slrrp.* I could just see Lucy folding her arms as she watched me trying to catch the little pieces falling from the sides of the burrito as I crunched into it.

I hadn't cracked a can of Diet Coke for millennia. I hurt my teeth when I mistakenly tried to bite into the top of the can. Rusty had gotten rusty. When I looked at the bewildered look on Nelsa's face as she saw me struggling with my drink, I realized how much simpler life with Lucy had been.

Finally, it came back to me. I hooked my finger under the aluminum lever and heard a pop. I'd apparently forgotten how refreshing a cold soda could be. I couldn't imagine how I'd done without it while wandering around as a hominid. Now Lucy's *slrrp, slrrp, slrrp* made literal sense. I imagined her licking her lips with her big tongue, one of her most famous gestures of approval.

When I finished, I asked Nelsa where to put the recyclables. How vulnerable her soft pink lips were as she purred with approval! I knew a lot of customers just threw cans in with the paper goods or left them on the counter for others to pick up. My considerate behavior was earning me points. I was trying my best to adhere to the tenets of the program and not behave like a sleazeball. But who knew? Maybe she and I would get it on when I returned from the primeval rain forest!

I was afraid to look at my reflection in the mirror, fearing the "time" I'd spent in the Pliocene era cavorting with Lucy would have impacted my morphology. I was pleasantly reassured that I was my same old self—still a stud millennial in tight-fitting designer jeans, my hair shaved at the sides so that the shock on the crown of my head looked a little like a toupee.

"Hasta la vista, baby," I mumbled after I paid.

Nelsa looked a little confused when I muttered under my breath, *Mayaa, mayaa, blx, blx,* which Google translator immediately rendered as "So long, it's been good to know you."

I finished off my burrito, washing it down with one last swig of my cold Diet Coke. Then I faced my reliable sandwich board and returned to Lucy—who was munching on a handful of berries as she waited patiently for my return as any pet might. I was so happy to see her, I literally jumped like an ape. Even though she had the hairy face of a gorilla, she was the girl of my dreams, at least the ones I was having as an *Australopithicus afarensis*. Parting definitely made the heart grow stronger.

She reminded me of a dog. Even though she plainly could relieve herself, she always walked in circles around me when I came back, as if she were waiting for me to take her out. Sometimes she would even lick my face, but she didn't like to kiss. Commenting on the species as a whole, I would have to say that in my experience the Australopithecus, like the *Homo erectus* who would follow, were not evolved enough for oral sex.

Seeing that I had never really experienced anything other than the perverse need to dominate my slaves, I wasn't sure if what I was experiencing with Lucy was love or just control. I wondered if I would have reacted any differently to her if she were just a vegetable or plant rather than an early ancestor of man.

I read a lot into her behavior. Would I have taken it as a come-on if a flower started to bloom on my return? Was fucking plant life comparable to fucking sheep? There was even an instance when I came upon a rose bush and suddenly felt myself grow so hard that I jumped and ended up scratching my dick on the thorns.

Most of our days were just spent foraging. While it's hard to reconstruct the argot of the Australopithecus, I wouldn't say that we discussed ideas. Sometimes when she looked at me and sighed, *Brrrrrrrrrr*, I thought it was like "I think therefore I am." But there was no doubt that she wasn't aware of being aware, or aware that one day she wouldn't be aware. I was sure she didn't really worry about the fact that some day she would die—in the way I did.

Once when I was going through a bad depression, I cried out the closest thing to "life is meaningless" in Australopithecanese. Lucy rubbed my leg and muttered, *Slc, slc, slc*, which loosely translated means "Stop feeling sorry for yourself."

I sensed she missed me when I went off into the bush to take a dump, and I was worried how she would react when at some point in the future she awakened to find I was no longer there—something which I knew would happen, despite putting it out of my mind.

Besides experiencing whatever it was we had—animal attraction, love, old-fashioned compatibility—this was the first time I'd ever lived with somebody. We enjoyed a rustic and bucolic existence and noshed all the time. I explained to Lucy that if she kept eating all day she would lose her appetite for dinner, something my parents were always warning me about when I was a kid. But she didn't listen. When I said such things, she just yawned *miyah*, which means what it sounds like—"Me, yeah!"

On the other hand, at dinnertime, we had to decide what to eat. If we found a hyena dining on the entrails of a giraffe, we were likely to join in. If I was more in the mood for hyena, I had to run all over town to locate the level of the food chain where a hyena might have met its match with a boa constrictor or feral pig.

The dinosaurs were long gone, but I kept hoping I could buddy up with some very strong creature who would take me under its wing and show me the ropes. After all, you never knew what was out there and who you were going to run into. There were times when I was afraid for my own safety.

But, as someone navigated the seamy side of life, I knew how to deal with tough guys. There were lots of gangs wandering the veldt. I would have loved to see the look on Lucy's face when I joined some once-extinct creature who had been grandfathered into existence. She would stomp up and down, yelling *djikes, djikes!* ("Go for it, baby!") as she watched me attack lions and tigers under the protection of the big boys on the block.

It was the same kind of fantasy of power I had with sex, but having a Tyrannosaurus Rex as a buddy would be a little like making friends with a tattooed biker alumnus in a maximum-security prison. I was just another short little Australopithecus guy, but if I had some friends in high places, I'd end up being able to pull strings and make sure we had the latest luxuries that Pliocene society had to offer.

Even without all the extinct creatures I used to see in the glass cases at the Museum of Natural History, I started to know my way around. Early ancestors of man like Australopithecus, *Homo erectus* and *Homo habilis* are really animals and still have a highly tuned sense of smell. Lucy was always scampering in the brush and she'd let out a triumphant *hrrrrmmph* as she emerged with something in her mouth. Once, I was even shocked to be confronted by the pornographic image of her gnawing on a dying creature's penis. I'd never seen anything like that, even in the raunchiest B&D loops, though it did bring back memories of John Wayne Bobbitt's wife Lorena. And some of my buddies would have been great oenophiles to the extent their sense of smell always led them to the best grapes.

I was also able to detect the level of pheromones in a way I couldn't when I was walking around midtown checking out all the skirts. This was like having X-ray vision. I could tell who was smoking hot and also where there would be rough riding. Even though we didn't discuss books, rock groups or movies, I knew more about Lucy than I'd known about any of the people in my life, including Jerry, Cliff, Tiffany, Muriel and even favorite slaves like Sonya and the ladyboy, Juanita.

I also felt that Lucy was the kind of gal who was on my team. Even though I might find her bending over backwards for another guy, she always seemed to want the best for me. She was a far cry from my mother who was critical and made me doubt myself. I had fond memories of her smiling with her big teeth then doing a little skip dance in which she landed on her back bicycling her legs—which I was sure she didn't perform for any of her other boyfriends.

I had to go back to the beginning of human life to relearn the basics. I pondered that maybe if I journeyed all the way back to the Big Bang, when the universe was created, I might come closer to the truest, most elemental form of the self. My only problem was, what to do about Lucy?

After all, the final goal of my travels was still to return to the version of my own life in a parallel universe where I would be caring and capable of having loving sexual relationships.

There were lots of logistics involved. Everyone else who knew me at the Wormhole Society and elsewhere would also be part of that parallel universe. Hence, they would be unable to appreciate the change, since they wouldn't have known me when I subjugated and degraded our fellow man (and women). I might even get to the point where, being such a standup fellow, I would forget what I had been in another dimension of space and time—something that could be dangerous.

Worms always reminded you that "you had a built-in forgetter" and that you had to "keep it green." Luckily, because those who traveled the multiverse had bifurcated consciousnesses and the ability to remember their previous lives, there was some degree of insurance—though I had heard stories about people who were in denial and started to go back to their old ways in spite of occupying new selves. It happened precisely because they forgot they possessed the propensity to deviate.

How would I explain the situation to Lucy, who didn't understand words like "forever?" My heart practically broke as I looked on her innocently dangling a banana between her legs. She let out a sigh as she fell asleep on a bed of palm fronds by the idyllic stream where we frolicked. An *Australopithecus afarensis* like her not only had no idea of the past or future, but she had also never journeyed more than a few miles from her favorite hunting grounds.

15

The Big Bang

Trying to explain my imminent departure to Lucy, in the language we both shared, was difficult. Australopithecanese contained no subjunctives. I jumped in the air and pointed to the sky. I cried *ho hoo*, which was how I called attention to something I wanted her to see. I waved my arm in the direction of a nearby stream, throwing a leaf in. I made her watch as it vanished in the current. I even climbed a tree, grabbing a vine and swinging dramatically to the ground like Tarzan. Since Lucy hadn't seen the movie, she didn't get the reference.

I couldn't decide if I would take off on such and such a day. This reminded me of my old basset hound. I couldn't face putting him to sleep until one day when he simply couldn't walk. Then I brought him to the vet who put him down. He knew exactly what I was up to, even if he didn't understand the ramifications, in their entirety.

I saw the same look in Lucy's eyes as we had our last meal of squirrel entrails, before our morning shag. I was sure she was going to break down as she lowered her face into the intestines of the animal, whose heart was still beating. I had the distinct feeling that *her* heart wasn't in it. She had lost her appetite.

Meeow, meow. Blixx. She almost sounded like a cat. We were cuddlers. The night before I left, as we spooned, I held her more tightly than ever, like a drowning man clinging onto dear life. She had to know in some part of her primitive psyche that I wasn't coming back when I walked off into the brush with my coconut, thinking hard about the sandwich board in front of the Downtown Cafe.

Lucy was as wonderful a specimen of an Australopithecanese woman as I was going to find anywhere. Yet I couldn't pretend feeling fulfilled sexually just because I was able to get it up without the usual S&M. It wasn't that we didn't share a common language. I could do without the usual shit about bands, flicks and clothes that millennials talk about, but I couldn't help feeling we were living an innocent lie. She couldn't understand me any more than I could her. I wasn't sure exchanging nuts and berries was the basis for a fulfilling life. Even if she could have gotten it, she was a very matter-of-fact type likely to have said the Australopithican equivalent of "Why go if you don't have to?" There wasn't much room for ideas in their tongue.

I was sure I heard a pathetic last cry from her, a sound somewhere between the Buddhist *ommmm* and an owl's hoot, as I finally took off.

I had already journeyed back to our earliest ancestors with Lucy being the mother of womankind. But being my usual extremist self, I figured I might as well go the whole route.

Naturally because of the Bang Bang Club, I always had the Big Bang on my mind. After all, isn't a state of cosmic coupling what we all are after in the end?

However, when I finally peered into the outset of time, nature's first orgasm didn't appear as some big white light. Rather it was like a cemetery, an impassive set of long flat stones that were barely perceptible in the darkness from which the slow ticking sound of a metronome emanated.

The beginning of everything reminded me of nothing.

If there had been some huge explosion, I might have stayed away, but as I descended back through the ages towards my new destination, past the age of dinosaurs and the newly formed Earth, to the creation of the solar system and beyond, I felt curiously removed. At first I figured I was on Prozac or some other SSRI, as my anxiety seemed to slip away, along with any vestiges of the flesh I once inhabited. It was as if my body had gone into shock after a trauma.

Did something come out of nothing? If I were caught in the ether or whatever was there before the creation of the universe, would the same space/time rules apply? Or is it possible that everything would be reduced to a minute quantum state? Would my existence be turned into pure energy or anti-matter in one fell swoop, rather than my corporeal essence continuing on as it had after the dawn of time? As an alumnus of the Bang Bang Club, I also couldn't help but wonder if the Big Bang lived up to its name. Was that what made me want to go back to it? Was it a porn flick with lots of facials and DP scenes, with the fireworks being a massive bukkake fest?

As it turned out, the Big Bang is a misnomer. The explosion was followed by a succession of pops that reminded me of the sound made by a bag of microwave popcorn. The day the first Higgs bosons blew into existence and matter was born was just like any other. Naturally, bosons don't perform the three S's—shit, shave and shower. You couldn't say the moment the universe came into being was like the beginning of a normal work week in Manhattan.

There were no sounds of taxis honking, garbage compactors or pneumatic drills opening the sidewalk. Even though it was the Big Bang, there was, of course, no Bang Bang Club or anything like it. It was a strictly PG-rated affair. For that matter, there was no Earth. If I were looking for a frame of reference, I would have to say it was a little like being stranded on some subway platform, anticipating the light from an oncoming train that never seems to come.

In that parallel universe my being was reduced to that of a subatomic particle in a state of continuous orgasm—though I must confess that one of the first feelings of panic I experienced when I landed back at the beginning of time with explosions going on all around me, was that I had no appendage with which to jerk off.

Still, even though I was a particle, rather than a sensate being, I looked on in wonder from that part of myself which still retained the faculty of consciousness. When I was a kid, I saw all kinds of simulations of the Big Bang at the old Hayden Planetarium. But the computer graphics didn't even begin to do justice to the experience of seeing the real thing.

First, bosons were the big boys on the block. Talk about Father Time…being a boson carried weight even without the Higgs soubriquet which would come 13.8 million years later, along with all the excitement about the Large Hadron Collider in Geneva. Being the grandaddy of all the other particles gives you some cachet, in addition to furnishing fodder if you're the kind of particle that has a lot of fantasies about sex with your more youthful counterparts. I looked like a faceless baby with my round bald pate and my rambunctious grabbing for everything that crossed my trajectory.

Being a boson, I was at the top of the food chain, but then the leptons lorded it over the muons, the neutrons and neutrinos, with the electrons being the heavyweights, the bouncers of the quantum world. And speaking of pre-ops, many of these particles were AC-DC—they flipped back and forth with their positive and negative charges. Besides the lack of gonads to grab onto, the one thing I hated the most about particles was the lack of pubic hair. The smooth surfaces gave me the eerie feeling that Brazilian waxing had originated with the creation of matter, and that smooth shaved surfaces were, sadly, the real "natural look." If you love Italian actresses of the '50s like Anna Magnani with their hairy armpits, then the Big Bang is not for you.

Did I want to hang around the dawn of time and be one of the bosons that were the early building blocks of life as we know it? The only love I would know in that world would derive from the kind of wham, bam, thank you ma'am kind of sex, the quantum entanglement that occurs when two particles, even those that are billions of light years apart, latch onto each other for the ultimate quickie. However, I felt a little like a serial killer aroused by the prospect of a potential victim standing in front of an open window. If I were looking for a real relationship, the Big Bang might be an example of "looking for love in all the wrong places," as the song goes.

Still, the answer turned out to be a fervent yes. My fellow particles were little emojis, who came at me with big smiles, then simply fused or split in a fission reaction. Even though you didn't have any time to get more than a glimmer of any one of them, I fell for the mysteriousness of these tiny particles that were gone almost as soon as you got to know one. There was one little muon I was hot on. Even though they were bald, I loved her curves; she was the elusive Scarlett Johansson of the quantum world. The B.B. (Big Bang) made the kind of collisions that go on in the Large Hadron Collider look like the difference between the softcore porn you see on Cinemax and the rough stuff you catch on 4chan. Colliding at the speed of light was what we did in our spare time. I knew that worms like myself, who were sensitive about being hit on, should definitely avoid the Big Bang. A real one-night stand would be an eternity in the B.B. and if, for instance, you were one of those particles that did get quantumly entangled with another particle, you were going make waves in a trillionth of a second. Promiscuity isn't the word for it. The B.B. was literally a quantum gangbang.

As I got to explore the lay of the land, I began to see that however magnificent the fireworks, I was going to have to get the hell out of there, unless I wanted to threaten my Wormhole recovery. The B.B. might have been where life started but it was no place to make a life. I could never get to know the particles with the positive charges the way I had Lucy. How was I going to settle down in a relationship, have kids and two cars in the garage with hot little particles hitting on me right and left?

One of my little quarks was multitasking. I always loved doing five things at once. I could have sex with a slave while cruising Tinder for fresh prey. I had this little perversion where I loved ordering in a Greek salad from a place like the Acropolis while also Greeking a ladyboy. The Big Bang was a multitasking paradise. I was a true social butterfly. Being such a light particle, I could perform my quantum entanglements with an almost unlimited number of partners at the same time and with the energy of a spermatozoa making its way up the fallopian tubes.

I might have missed the simple unselfconscious existence I led with Lucy back in the Pliocene era, but I had to admit taking on the identity of a subatomic particle at the time of the Big Bang was really a blast—even if my selfie would have looked like little more than the exhaust that fighter jets leave in a blue summer sky.

Essentially, I was having a very enjoyable slip, which I could continue until the cows came home or in this case until the 4.5 billion years when the solar system began to form. I was on a furlough from the program. I was hitting on other particles and they were coming on to me. When you get bombarded enough, you're going to lose the sense of feeling whole. Rather than finding myself, I was losing it in a truly Zen way. I desperately needed a meeting, particularly in one instance where I hooked up with a really hot muon. When I say hot, I mean over a million degrees.

I might have been footloose and fancy free. I might have consoled myself that it was literally impossible to apply the principles of the program in a quantum universe where someone coming on to you at the speed of light was business as usual. I could convince myself that my mysterious Scarlett Johansson muon was not a person, but a particle that behaved according to laws different than the ones I was familiar with in the world from which I had come. But when we collided something really happened. We were hardly passing each other like ships in the night.

Infinitely small bits of matter and energy created relationships in equally infinitesimal periods of time. They swirled towards me like a great ballroom dancer. I lifted them off the little tentacles that passed for feet amongst these massless sprites. If only for a trillionth of second, we were really a couple. There was one time I remember quite clearly when we talked breathlessly to each other like Rick and Lisa in *Casablanca* while the B.B. equivalent of "As Times Goes By" played in the background.

"Here's looking at you, kid," I told her before we vanished before each other's eyes. I wasn't going to brunch with her, but even trading in tiny fractions of a second, there was still a subtext. It was hard to remember particles I had met in the billions of interchanges that I experienced at any moment. I can say with certainly that most quantum matter is transparent—especially when it comes to hooking up.

"You're only as sick as your secrets" is one of the credos of the Wormhole Society. I didn't have the feeling that neutrinos or even big swaggering electrons, who were the larger-than-life NBA players of the microcosm, were keeping anything from me. But I had to admit that my whole existence with these fast movers was fueling my denial. As much fun as I was having, it was going to be hard finding what I was looking for.

The birth of life was a dark matter. With all the almost imperceptible possibilities coming at you, it was literally like finding a needle in a haystack, a cosmic one at that. The nice part was that I wasn't going to have to feel guilty about saying goodbye to anyone since I had so many partners.

In the quantum universe, where you could be in two places at the same time, things like cheating, breaking up or even leaving weren't dramatic life changes. I wasn't going to miss a subatomic mate the way I had my Lucy.

The wormhole I entered when I departed the Big Bang was very much like the Large Hadron Collider in Geneva. Heading back towards my apartment on First Avenue, I had the same feeling of being bombarded day and night until finally I caved in and gave up my psychic attachment to that first Higgs boson from which human life would eventually evolve and in which my being had temporarily resided.

None of the journeys take time, which is precisely the point. Yet this one felt long and steep enough to create the sensation I once had ascending the Cyclone at Coney Island. You climbed slowly to the top. Then came a hair-raising fall that ended with you yelling out with a mixture of fear and relief when you landed back in the present. It must have sounded like a cry for help; several people plucked phones from their pockets as if they were going to call the cops, even though no one was chasing me and I plainly wasn't in any danger.

I ran upstairs to the apartment fearing that paramedics might come and take me away in a straitjacket. They certainly would have if I explained I was simply irritable and overtired after the long journey home from the beginning of time.

16

Gwen

Two hands slammed down on my shoulders. Then I was pulled roughly off the ground.

"Ow!"

"Ow's about thee, lad? 'hat makes thee in yon fir." The words sounded like an indecipherable Scottish brogue, the kind of Edinburgh argot I remembered from *Trainspotting*.

"Help! Somebody help!" I yelled.

I suddenly remembered that women were instructed to yell "Fire," as loud as they could when they were being assaulted by rapists.

"Fire!" I screamed frantically. "I'm being kidnapped against my will."

I realized I was being redundant. Nobody is willingly kidnapped.

It was taking a while, but now as I came to from the blow to my head with which Mark Twain begins his famous novel, I was beginning to get it. In the parallel universe I'd landed in, I was *a Connecticut Yankee in King Arthur's court!*

Indeed, I was wearing wide wale corduroy overalls, a vest and worn leather boots that laced up to the ankle. I was speaking an English that made as little sense to my captors as it would to me once I had become firmly ensconced in my newest reality.

As my hands were clamped in irons, a rope was strung around my waist so I could be pulled along by my captor's donkey. Nevertheless, I devised a plan.

Yankees were famous for their ingenuity and cleverness and were known for their wiles. But the minute I tried to explain myself and tell everyone I was visiting from a place called Connecticut where I worked in a big factory, it only made matters worse.

I could tell that horses were status symbols back then—the way cars are today. The fact that I didn't have one only made me look more like some kind of a lowlife or crazy person. In medieval times, to be crazy was to be inhabited by the devil.

Once I was put in my goal, which was what they called jail, I got wind of the fact that I would not be long for this world. My gaoler was Little John, who despite his name was in fact a giant. He was the first person in Camelot who took pity on me, but it was he who informed me my captors were gathering the hay they laid under the wood when someone was about to be burned at the stake.

I had been suffering from a good case of worm lag. Twenty hours to Tokyo or Bangkok is considered a long flight, but I had literally traversed billions of years to get to my destination and was feeling pretty bombed out.

I had a dream in which a muon that looked just like one of the ghosts chasing Pac-Man was entangled with another boson. I woke up with a twinge of regret about no longer being an early building block of life. If I weren't me, who was they?

Someone at a meeting once said, "The ego will die." I realized I had to be careful not to abuse my wormholing abilities. I might not have been George Washington if I wormholed back to a parallel universe in 1776, but I could easily have been reincarnated as one of the early signers of the Declaration of Independence. Who knew if I were

Alexander or even Catherine the Great, the noble woman said to have fucked her horse?

I might have ended up royalty or at the very least a big shot. Maybe not one of the queens I ran into at the Bang Bang or even as I was finding out now, A CONNECTICUT YANKEE IN KING ARTHUR'S COURT!

However, I decided to go along for the ride. Maybe I was where I was supposed to be and I would find the innocent sexuality I sought. Neither King Arthur nor his knights would have heard of the Big Bang or even needed the kind of submissive types you found in a place like the Bang Bang Club to get it up. That's why they called it Camelot. It was there that I would learn the codes of chivalry which would lead me to finding romantic love.

I stopped dead in my tracks. I had only recently picked up a tattered copy of *Connecticut Yankee* along with a bunch of *National Geographic* lying with some other garbage outside my building on First Avenue. And now the words came back to me:

> ***"You know about transmigration of souls; do you know about transposition of epochs—and bodies?"***

Connecticut Yankee is a tale within a tale in which the narrator finds a manuscript, but my head started to spin when I discovered direct reference to the act of wormholing within the original. Had I inadvertently fallen into yet another wormhole where I was a character in a book? Was Twain himself a Worm?

Over the infinity of time and space there certainly was no problem finding a parallel universe in which I was reborn as the hero of a novel I'd loved as a kid. I could recall escaping into *Connecticut Yankee* just as I was now being lured into a magical new part of the multiverse where fiction became reality.

"Camelot—Camelot," said I to myself. "I don't seem to remember hearing of it before. Name of the asylum, likely.'

It was a soft, reposeful summer landscape, as lovely as a dream, and as lonesome as Sunday. The air was full of the smell of flowers, and the buzzing of insects, and the twittering of birds, and there were no people, no wagons, there was no stir of life, nothing going on. The road was mainly a winding path with hoof-prints in it, and now and then a faint trace of wheels on either side in the grass—wheels that apparently had a tire as broad as one's hand.

So, I found myself waking up as the character of Hank Morgan. I was an engineer from Hartford transported 1,300 years back to Camelot. I could see a castle in the distance, which I immediately thought was the Cloisters in Washington Heights.

I had a similar thing happen only a short while before when I'd dropped some acid during a clusterfuck at the Bang Bang. I came down from the trip behind Cleopatra's Needle in Central Park.

It had been a dazzlingly beautiful morning, much like the one I was experiencing now. Here in medieval times, I found myself squinting as I came upon a group of knights in shining armor who looked like they were about to joust. Not totally absorbing the idea that I really landed here (and that this was not some dream from which I would eventually awaken), I figured I simply had come upon one of those Renaissance fairs where people dress up in armor and involve themselves in live-action role playing or, as it's called, LARPing. Perhaps I had stumbled onto the set of an episode of *Game of Thrones*.

I also imagined that the knights on horseback might simply be New York City cops in Central Park. Maybe the costumed characters that included maypole dancers were just a gambit to fool the drug dealers who were always plying their trade on the Sheep Meadow. For a moment I believed the music was some weird new band with a medieval theme, until I saw the drums and the old-fashioned fifes with their long stems blown by a marching band of troubadours wearing oversized velvet caps and billowing embroidered culottes.

I decided it was a waste to give up after having perfected my wormholing to such an extent that I had turned myself into a literary classic. If I disappeared and returned they would surely judge me a warlock, or another entity with magical powers. And who knew how easy it would be to find my way back once I returned to the present? I had achieved it with Lucy, but it isn't easy to leave and then wormhole yourself back to the exact same coordinates. Wormholing is haphazard and sloppy in some ways, since what goes through your mind has such an influence on the success of your "flight." You could hardly call it an exact science or, for that matter, a science at all.

But I had to take a chance, there was no other choice. I didn't want to die in the past. I pretended to look hard into Little John's eyes as he brought me the bowl of gruel that would likely be my last meal. Instead of the image of myself reflected on his retina I conjured up my old adorable friend and my best pal in the multiverse—the sandwich board of the Downtown Cafe. The connection from Camelot was very good. I could almost instantaneously see the list of the day's specials, which immediately made my mouth water: enchiladas with ground meat chili peppers and green sauce, a beef burrito with mole and cheese quesadilla made with Monterey Jack. At least I knew there remained an out, if I got into even deeper trouble.

I hadn't eaten since before I left for King Arthur's court. My hunger only intensified my homesickness, the vacuum of my empty stomach sucking on the time barrier to the point where my departure was like the kind of explosion you experience when you've been jerking yourself off without coming, the act of edging that is so popular among the metrosexuals of the twenty-first century.

I looked at the specials on the sandwich board as soon as I arrived back with the usual swishing sound that finished with an idling of my inner engine.

Nelsa was behind the counter as usual, but I was disappointed that I wasn't getting a ticker-tape parade down Broadway. I felt like Odysseus, who was recognized only by his dog Argos when he returned home after many years on the lam. But you have to be grateful for little things. Her taking me for granted only proved that time itself was working with the proficiency of a Swiss clock.

I hadn't disturbed anything more traveling thirteen centuries into the past than I had going back thirteen billion years to the advent of being.

"What'll it be today?" she said. "We're out of the burrito with the mole sauce."

I thought of pulling a quick one—eating and then running for it. But I didn't know if my departure from the past would be noted any more than my departure from the present had been. I needed to find the exact right chink in time to make my point. If they had already lighted the fires that would be used to burn me at the stake, I'd be in good shape. But if I came back too soon, I would simply land in my cell, a strange creature howling about the multiverse in a language that no one understood. Parallel universes are a fragile thing. There are ones filled with other Lucys, who not only do not miss me but have no inkling of my very existence. So I ordered the chicken quesadilla that is always a reliable choice.

"Ice cold Diet Coke," Nelsa said, plopping a can on the counter. "Just the way you like it."

She recognized me after all! How I could have missed how attractive she was with her beautiful ass, dramatic shock of glistening dark hair and piercing blue eyes. Behind the tough façade, she plainly knew how to cater to a man's desires. But you don't want to shit where you eat, literally in this case. I was still amazed I hadn't even once tried to offer her money to come upstairs when my kennel was running strong. I realized the wrong buttons were being pushed when I caught myself regressing to having fantasies about her naked and caged in a dog crate with a studded collar around her neck.

I would have hit a meeting but I was in a rush to get back to Camelot.

If lucky, I could time this whole thing perfectly. I would arrive just as the flames were being stoked for my immolation. They of course would wonder where I had gone. If they interpreted my disappearance as more evidence of sorcery, I'd have to hightail it out of there all over again, taking my frustration out on the beautiful naked butt of Nelsa who I now imagined bending over her griddle.

"Would you like guacamole or sour cream?" she asked.

I was like one of those prisoners on death row having their last supper. And it was a particularly good one at that since the quesadilla had been grilled with the kind of TLC that made me start to think maybe Nelsa was the one. Here I am travelling through recorded and unrecorded time seeking the perfect partner who can make me hard again (and in the meantime even learning something about love) when the solution to all my problems is no further than my own backyard or, in this case, door. I knew I was on a mission for which no shirking of responsibility could be possible. When I finished quaffing down the quesadilla with a huge gulp of soda, I ran outside and looked up First Avenue, afraid that if I got too comfortable, I might just sit there all-day eating quesadillas, fantasizing about Nelsa and ultimately losing my resolve.

"Jeepers, sorry, that's a long tale," I found myself saying. I never had used the word "jeepers" in my whole life, but I quickly realized that I was talking like a character out of a nineteenth century novel by a famed American humorist.

"Hark, good man. Where art thou go to?"

Little John showed concern and even worry, but it was plain he was mostly confused. He didn't understand a good part of what I had told him, which concerned the plant in Hartford where I worked, the kind of firearms we manufactured and the accident that was responsible for my ending up in Camelot.

I stupidly tried to explain that there was no sense in trying to burn me at the stake since I wasn't even a real person, but a character in literature. However, I'd already come and gone. Little John was beginning to get the idea he had better take me seriously, if only to save his own hide when it turned out I was still able to vanish—even as I was going up in flames.

I noticed Little John had also enlisted the services of a chap I later learned was a disciple of Merlin the magician. He was a dour-looking fellow who uttered all kinds of odd-sounding chants in the face of the miracle I'd performed in eluding death.

"I can help you, kind sir," he said with a respectful tone. "I'm an alchemist!"

"Mark Twain weren't even his real name, I said. "That just refers to the depth of the Mississippi. He was really Samuel Clemens."

"Ye said ye were Hank."

He grabbed me by the scruff of my neck, but in a friendly way. Before I knew it, I was passing the stake. A rather comely witch was next in line.

She let out a shrill scream, which I'm ashamed to say turned me on. I would share about it at the meeting.

Then, there I was at the court, which reminded me of my experience of being arraigned for pandering. Little John was my arresting officer. I waited my turn to plead our case to the judge who in his case turned out to be the king himself.

I figured I would treat it like any sales situation.

"Hank Morgan," I said holding out my hand.

It was plain shaking hands was not yet a salutation in the sixth century. The courtiers rushed in to block my way. I quickly pulled my hand back so that I eventually stood before the king much in the way I imagined a Yankee like Hank Morgan would hang around in Hartford, with my hands in the back pockets of my trousers.

"Arthur," he said.

"Not the..." I replied in amazement, before nervously blurting out. "I had an uncle Arthur."

He had a bemused smile as he bent his hand before my face. From reading about the round table as a kid, I remembered you got down on your knees, kissing the hand that had been held out to you.

"And ye hearken from whence?"

"Actually, I hearken from a work of fiction by Mr. Mark Twain."

I would have continued but, having been an English major back in college, I remembered that the novel form hadn't been invented until the fourteenth century. I could have shown my smarts by talking about the work that's generally considered to be the first novel in Western literature—Thomas Mallory's *Le Morte d'Arthur*. But present company considered, I didn't think that would go over too big.

"Greet thy queen, strange man," he continued. "Say hello to Guinevere."

I knew she was supposed to be beautiful but Gwen, as I would call her, was a little dowdy for my taste. From what I could see, none of the women in the kingdom knew how to dress. They all wore long embroidered gowns with rug-thick material that hid everything.

My father always said "say hello to" this one or that. I rebelled by inserting a comma and quotes after the say. Now that Arthur was just beginning to get the impression I was for real (and that I might be able to help him even more than Merlin and the other shysters and mountebanks who were already glaring enviously at me), I was getting cocky. As it appeared I was being spared, I was positioning myself to show my cards. Everyone would see that the new kid on the block had some smarts.

"Hello to Guinevere," I intoned

We were in the heart of the industrial revolution in Connecticut. As I looked at Arthur decked out in his crown and heavy pendants, I thought about the basic principles of economy of scale and division of labor. How could these be applied?

I could see that except for the occasional burning at the stake, life moved at a snail's pace. One of the first things I was going to suggest was replacing the scribe with one of the new stenographers who had recently become all the craze back in Hartford, or at least someone who could take down basic dictation with a lead pencil. I would dispose of the broken-down old wretch they currently employed, who still relied on the laborious and time-consuming process of dipping his feather in ink.

And it was not only that. Steam turbines and electricity were fast replacing tapers and kerosene lamps. The town had been changing overnight. What if Camelot didn't even have to endure a gas-lit era? What if the carts carrying the poor wretches to burn at the stakes could be motorized, so they could be put out of their misery as fast as possible? Being an engineer I was aware that, by the dawn of the twentieth century, the gallows would be replaced by an electric chair.

I had to figure out where to start. How could I get my ideas across to Arthur when I got to the famous roundtable? I didn't want to freeze up in front of Launcelot and the other knights. I was sure they were going to poke holes in my story—with their swords!

"Prithee," I extracted a box of matches from my pocket and pulled out my pipe. I stuffed some tobacco from my leather pouch into the bowl which hung from the pipe's elegant, curved stem. I looked around to make sure there wasn't a "No Smoking" sign before lighting up.

Arthur could be a tough ass. He was a warrior, but for a king he also had an avuncular side; he seemed to enjoy the fact that I was relaxing and trying to make myself at home before delivering my spiel.

He pointed to a cushioned chair that stood against one of the stone pillars supporting the auspicious-looking, high-vaulted ceiling that soared over the court. I rushed to bring it to him.

"Hark," he said holding his scepter up in the air. His vassals in their leotards and funny-looking hats jumped and moved the chair closer to me. I was being treated like a king! It was amazing how quickly my fortunes had changed. It was like night and day.

Merlin scowled as a courtier brought over the chair, placing it not ten feet from Arthur. The courtier fluffed the cushion. He bent his head obsequiously as he waved his arm in the direction of the seat and backed away.

"Your highness," I began to mimic how I thought people addressed Queen Victoria in Mark Twain's time.

Arthur and Gwen rolled their eyes. There were whispers amongst the courtiers, followed by a hush. I was struggling to determine how to express that I could introduce innovations that would save their realm a ton of money. I didn't want to oversell, but I knew I had some bankable ideas. There were also things like the Napoleonic Code by which Arthur could increase the feeling of his power and presence even in the farthest reaches of his realm.

I remembered that they were in the middle of a war, the Crusades, in which Launcelot and the other knights sought the Holy Grail.

Arthur motioned toward Merlin, who came forward surrounded by two acolytes carrying a smoking cauldron by its handles. They looked like they were on the verge of having an accident. The cauldron was placed right at Merlin's feet so that the smoke rose in front of his face. There was something frightening about it, but I told myself I was a man of science and would not let myself be intimated by a charlatan who was no more than a clown.

Back in Connecticut he would be lucky to get hired by one of those traveling carnivals with the bearded women. Even as a magic show, this was fairly primitive. I had already performed my match trick when I lit the pipe, so I was running out of gags. I could talk all I wanted about steam turbines and electricity, but it all would fall on deaf ears. Unless I had something concrete, I would be in no position to challenge Merlin's seniority as a sorcerer.

And then it hit me.

When I said, "Your highness," Arthur looked down at his throne, to see how far my words brought him up from the ground. The whole court exploded in laughter. I was confused at first but then I joined in, roaring along with the rest of them.

I stepped forward and whispered to Arthur and Gwen that I needed Merlin to come forward. I explained that if Merlin could be given twenty or even thirty apprentices, the kingdom would now have the beginnings of an army of magicians whose powers could be used to both vanquish the enemy and fill the coffers of the royal treasury.

"Gold," I said. "With the help of all these magicians Merlin will turn base metal into gold."

I was employing the basic principles of industrial production— division of labor and economy of scale— that I had used as manager of a factory in Hartford. Before you knew it, your thirty Merlin clones would teach thirty more and you'd have 900 Merlins. Those 900 would become 2,700 plus 930 to make a total of 3,630, and so forth. Soon enough a virtual army of magicians would ramp up the magical powers at work in the kingdom, just the way the steam turbines in the factory became an increasing source of energy as they grew bigger and more powerful.

By employing my old Yankee ingenuity, I disarmed Merlin. If you're going to be a usurper, you don't want to look like one. The relatively new sport of baseball had just come to Hartford. I had thrown good old Merlin a curve. How was he supposed to vilify the person who would increase the amount of respect and adulation he was accorded? When I was done, his magic wonders would penetrate into every little hamlet of then not so Great Britain.

As I watched Merlin's chest swell under his chainmail, I felt sorry he had to sweat in excitement under such heavy attire.

"My friend Merlin's whole army of magicians will spare you from the Moor."

At that the gallery went into a frenzy with wild cheering and banners waving. Timing is everything. I was waiting for the right moment and got lucky.

I spotted some gold dust which I figured had dropped from one of the courtier's pockets. In my first appearance before the king, I quickly convinced all of my Midas touch by using a piece of rock I found on the ground, which luckily had magnetic properties, to collect the dust.

The rock was cupped tightly in my palm. Swinging my fist to the ground and then swiftly into the air, there was a great cry of awe as the gold rained down on Arthur and Guinevere.

"And there's more, much more where that came from, my gracious king."

"But Hank, you're truly a wizard," exclaimed Arthur.

I was pleased the King and I were now on a first name basis. Building a friendly trusting relationship is the first principle of all sales.

I needed to hammer the nail in the coffin. Since it was growing dark, I summoned Arthur and his whole retinue outside to the castle's courtyard.

"And now behold the heavens," I cried out.

Merlin grimaced. The envy of my powers caused him great mental anguish. I wondered if he was experiencing a migraine.

My luck had been uncanny. I advanced my cause at my rival's expense. I correctly calculated that Halley's Comet would appear on the evening of my first audience—September 7, 607. And there it was, right on cue, dramatically streaking across the sky over the castle. There was another round of gasps and expressions of awe, followed by cheers rising from the gallery.

I had gone from death row to being a trusted royal advisor within a matter of minutes.

I was just following one of the great showmen of all time, John Ringling, whose circus came regularly to the Atheneum in Hartford. By calling attention to Merlin and the possible expansion of his operation, I was riding a wave, in which I, as the bringer of good news, became the center of attention.

Merlin had slinked out of sight. I saw him cowering in the shadows of a pillar. But he had to put up or shut up. I was already becoming quite a celebrity. When and if he couldn't or wouldn't step up to the plate, I'd grab his scepter. My powers may have come from science and progress, but I had no intention of disabusing anyone of the notion that I—as a producer of magic wonders—had a direct connection to God.

I noticed Arthur nodding his head as if in agreement with what Gwen was saying as she whispered in his ear. Then Arthur motioned for me to advance. For a moment, I feared losing control of my bladder. His throne sat on a pedestal. There was only so far I could go. When I ventured as close as I had seen any of the royal courtiers approach him, Gwen beckoned to me vigorously as if she were, say, on a train about to depart the station after the conductor had just cried "all aboard." I stumbled as I ran towards the throne and bent down on one knee as I had seen others do—before Arthur impatiently motioned me close enough so no one else could hear.

Even though it's never supposed to happen, I crossed the time barrier in mid-sentence. I was no longer Hank Morgan but Rusty Russianoff, as I exclaimed under my breath, FUCKING A! KING ARTHUR IS WHISPERING INTO MY FUCKING EAR. I'M GRATEFUL

FOR NOT BEING ABLE TO GET IT UP. IF I WERE STILL ABLE TO GET IT UP BY DEGRADING SUBMISSIVE WOMEN AND LADYBOYS, I WOULD NEVER HAVE MET FUCKING KING ARTHUR AND HAD HIM WHISPERING IN MY FUCKING EAR. TALK ABOUT TURNS-ONS.

The only problem was that, in my excitement, I had agreed without really understanding what had been said. Suddenly, I heard a fife and drums as Arthur's knights strode into the court. From the upper balconies colorful purple and maroon banners dramatically unfolded.

I stood up and found myself leading a procession right out of the court onto a large field where several jousting matches were already taking place. I stopped as one young knight, thrown from his horse, opened his visor and screamed in pain as he clutched at his leg.

"He'll need a splint and will end up in a cast," I announced.

My consorts smiled at me indulgently. I was now somewhat of a presence in the court, but that obviously didn't stop them from thinking I was nuts. A little further on, Merlin was standing in front of a large cauldron, getting ready to perform his "double, double toil and trouble" act.

In the distance Gwen rode sidesaddle towards me.

"Mommy!" I cried, in the involuntary way that students do in grade school. My face turned red with shame. But the embarrassment passed almost as soon as it came. Thankfully there were none of the guffaws that accompanied these outbursts when I was a kid.

There had been a few of us who lost control like this and even pissed ourselves. We were constantly picked on and bullied for these lapses, which was really no more than early-onset Tourette Syndrome.

"Hank!" called Gwen.

I noticed she was wearing a revealing bodice. She was a blonde, which made me see her in a totally different light than I had at court. There with her face, neck and head covered, she looked like a nun. I wasn't quite sure how to address a famous historical figure like Queen Guinevere, but I thought "to thine own self be true." I'd handle it the way any Connecticut Yankee would, hailing her arrival by crying out, "Hey there, Gwen!"

"Hound's blood, knave!" yelled a knight. "She's the queen!"

I had been protecting myself from any disrespect by thinking they wouldn't recognize the nickname. As far as the Queen or anyone was concerned, "Gwen" could just be another one of the barely comprehensible things I was saying. But I was obviously wrong.

She dismounted from her horse and smiled indulgently, as I looked right down into her blouse, getting a locker room-style view of her coffee-colored aureoles.

"Allow Sir Hank to pass," she said, addressing the knight.

Her horse lowered his big dick and pissed in the dirt.

We both stared for a moment, but I knew better than to reveal my feelings since "fuck's" roots go back to Middle English. The last thing I needed was for her to take offense at my cursing.

I had no idea of the mores of Camelot or if the aristocracy screwed around, but she was the one who would have to make the first move. In all this time travel you never really know how people behave. I had only breezed over Victorian England. Despite it being an era that was said to be very uptight, I knew from reading the dirty passages in Steven Marcus's *The Other Victorians* that I would have to watch out if I didn't want to be triggered.

Was Camelot also a promiscuous place? Back in the '60s, the Kennedy White House, also called Camelot, was a virtual whorehouse. Jack had famously watched his pal getting a blowjob from an amanuensis. But Hartford in the nineteenth century was pretty puritanical. The only whorehouses my Hank Morgan persona would have heard about existed way out west in a town like the fictional

Dodge City, where Miss Kitty sold her favors on Gunsmoke.

Even so, I was taken aback when Gwen laughed heartily as she grabbed the horse's dick and hauled up her skirts. I had heard all the rumors about Catherine the Great's equine antics, but it was nothing compared to the sight of Gwen accommodating her Trigger. "Cunt" was another word that came from Middle English. It meant "the valley where two hills meet." But she was still the queen. I wasn't about to discuss linguistics in the middle of her orgasm. She emitted a piercing scream as she came, then pulled down her skirts as if nothing untoward had happened.

The howls of approval from a group of courtiers in the distance let me know that the local mores were a far cry from the brand of Plymouth Rock puritanism we practiced back at home.

The mixture of Gwen's cries sounding like the ululations of a cat, and the naying of her horse, reminded me of our beloved Hartford Zoo where I'd once witnessed the consummation of the love affair between two baboons. However, Gwen was all business. Staring brazenly into the faces of her courtiers, she made it apparent she was simply showing her skill in some kind of sporting event. Lucy would have fit right in since, even with the advent of Christianity, men and women still behaved like animals.

I thought I was seeing things when Gwen locked her gaze on me. At first I had an attack of the old performance anxiety. Though I had heard about guys who were hung like horses, how was I going to compete with one? I had to remind myself that I was Hank Morgan, a character out of a novel, and not Rusty Russianoff, a recovering Worm who treated women like dogs in order to conquer his fear of sex.

Before I knew it, Gwen yanked up her skirts again and flung herself at me. Her horse was remarkably human; even though he had already taken a pee, he pissed again, as I did after a fuck. He also began to fart. The problem was that I was on the ground with Gwen, totally unaware of the puddle of urine inching toward us, as she valiantly rode me. I also had to contend with the river of horse ejaculate leaking out of the Queen, just as I was on the way in. It was like trying to paddle against a strong current.

Happily, I discovered I'd found yet another period of history in which I was totally functional. I had no difficulty getting it up, even though I was now in the submissive rather than dominant position—not to speak of the fact that I had to endure the barn-like smell that became more pronounced as I penetrated my new lover.

Even though I might have been freed from a pattern of treating my sex partners like slaves, I wasn't able to enjoy the feeling of success because of my anxiety about the encroaching river of piss. Already a little conversant with court etiquette, I was going to have a lot of explaining to do if I interrupted a Queen just as she was about to come.

Even whilst she yelled wildly for her "Artie" as she bounced with complete abandon up and down on my member, I dug furiously at the ground beside us, managing to create a small trench into which the stallion's bladder harmlessly emptied.

Here was an example where my engineering training came in handy. I began to think that one of my contributions to the realm might lie in using my talents to improve the sewage system, which was notoriously poor in medieval England. We Hartford residents had numerous safety checks that insured against coitus interruptus because of errant horse piss, the most effective of which was our advanced sewage system.

When she finished having her way with me, Gwen stuck a piece of sugar in my mouth. Then she slapped me on my ass before she jumped back on her steed, galloping off into the field of vermillion banners with a self-satisfied smile. I could hear the roar of her knights and the clanking of chain mail as the crowd parted to make way for their queen.

I have never run for any elective office, but my character Hank had something to do with Republican politics in Connecticut, having campaigned heartily for the current mayor. So, I knew that scandal was the least thing you needed to get involved with. Even though it wasn't my fault, I started to kick myself for having sex with such a prominent person. Not only did I run the risk of disfavor with Arthur, but also by going all the way with Gwen, I was now in danger of fomenting her ire. What if I fell for someone else? Hell knows no fury...." What would I do if I were caught in a situation where Arthur needed me, but Gwen demanded my attentions in bed? Who knew what was going on in their relationship? What if she started to like me better than him? I might have been spared being burned at the stake, but my goose ran a good chance of getting cooked.

Then I heard the hooves of a horse galloping behind me. I turned to find Arthur himself, with both a lance and scabbard in hand. I don't know how he was doing it. Maybe it was Merlin's magic, but he was also twirling an iron ball affixed to a chain. Launcelot was not far behind. As he rapidly approached, he pulled down the visor of his helmet so that I could no longer see his face.

Was this how it was all going to end? I wildly tried to conjure up the sandwich board of the Downtown Cafe and the comforting visage of Nelsa pushing a sweaty can of Diet Coke in my direction. My adrenalin must have been on overdrive. Nothing would work. I was reminded of the panic that sets in when you start to lose a hard-on. I intoned Jerry's advice—"You can't will an erection." I hoped that this suggestion about how to handle a limp dick would also free my mind.

"Help!" I intoned aloud. "Time for this one to come home…"

Then I found myself on the corner of Fourth Street and First Avenue, standing in front of the equine form of one of New York's Finest, who also happened to be taking a leak. To say that he was well hung would be a euphemism, though the wonderful thing about horses is that they have little ego when it comes to these matters. They don't compare and despair.

The big dick reminded me of the snakes that plumbers use to clear out a clogged pipe. Unbeknownst to its rider, the horse proceeded to hose down the street, which looked like one of those cleanups following a street fair.

It was nice to know that some things never changed. Just like Gwen's horse, its eyes looked totally blank and free of any signs of satisfaction with itself as it took a major dump while the river of piss made its way toward my feet.

I stepped up on the curb, clearing a little space in the drain with a discarded brush. The mounted officer looked nonplussed. My managerial skills were coming in handy again, in precisely the way they had when I dug a trench in the field.

"Sorry, force of habit," I explained, in time to watch the threatening puddle flow neatly into the drain—an invention that was an improvement from medieval times and something that Gwen and I would have profited from if I'd happened to be fucking her in the gutter, where sadly most of my thoughts still seemed to lie.

At first I thought I was back for just a couple of days of R and R. I would hit some meetings. But Gwen and her horse whet my juices. I toyed with the idea of taking a little vacation from sobriety and hitting the Bang Bang. I even contemplated ordering a hot young ladyboy from Dial-a-Slave. The meetings would always be there. I still had a compulsive need to see if I could get a hard-on now that I was back in the twenty-first century. Looking for the easy out, I figured I'd opt for some controlled depravity and maybe attend orgies just once or twice a week.

However, moderation wasn't one of my strongpoints.

One party led to another. I was right back where I'd left off. Only the depredations were more intense. I sought out even more desperate characters than Sonya, whores who'd do anything for a hit of meth. I demanded even more debasement from my slaves. Before I knew it, I was on the Stroll picking up rent boys (and girls) at all hours of the day and night. I stole their French fries too.

Fortunately, I'd landed back at the very start of the #MeToo era. I'd pay a price for my compulsive behavior and the consequences would likely be more severe.

17

Nelsa

I was indulging but also planning my next descent into the wormhole—to escape.

The morning after one of these binges, I woke up, threw on a pair of jeans and a T-shirt and stumbled into the Downtown Cafe. Nelsa, in her tight purple spandex pants and pointed high heels, was pushing the tables to the side so she could mop the floor. The place smelled like a peep show due to the bucket of disinfectant that sat on a dolly.

She wore a tight black T-shirt with a plunging neckline that tantalizingly outlined her cleavage.

I found that when I started to get really keyed up, I suffered from a kind of erotomania that made me feel everyone desired me.

I was sure Nelsa was looking suggestively upwards towards my apartment and then downwards at my package, as I perused the daily specials.

We always talked and joked. She looked up to me as if I were an older brother who was going somewhere in life. I don't know how she got the idea into her head. I didn't dress for success. I certainly wasn't one of those NYU students who were increasingly populating Alphabet City.

One day before I took off for Camelot, I was standing in front of the building when Meryl Streep appeared out of nowhere, her face partially hidden by a large hat. She was looking for the Theater for the New City. I pointed her in the right direction.

Nelsa had been watching me through the window of the restaurant. That must have solidified her impression that I was somebody. After all, the East Village is full of up-and-coming actors, directors and producers. For all she knew, I could be the Martin Short of tomorrow.

For Nelsa, it was just another day with its burritos and quesadillas. For me, travelling through time in a wormhole was not like going to California or Europe. You didn't think of yesterday when wandering around Beverly Hills or the Champs-Elysées, since there was no yesterday and no tomorrow.

Even if she maintained the erroneous idea that I knew famous Hollywood actresses, Nelsa would never have dreamed that I had been fucking King Arthur's wife, as Launcelot and the Knights of the Round Table galloped by on horseback. This type of sex tourism was the kind of thing you could only share at Wormhole meetings, where no one would have batted an eyelid.

Nelsa gyrated her booty to the beat of salsa playing on a Latino radio station. Her shiny jet-black hair was pulled back tightly in a braid which was the perfect rein for the bit I couldn't help imagining between her teeth.

She locked on you with her imploring, dark eyes. She was the kind of woman who wasn't afraid to show her hand. She knew what she wanted.

Considering what I'd been through I wasn't hungry, but I ordered the ham and avocado salad special just to make conversation. When she bent down to bring my order to me, at the table right next to a cupboard full of Goya products, I looked around to make sure no one was looking, then planted a kiss right on the lips.

I figured it was progress compared to what I used to do in the presence of a woman whose anatomy was calling out to me. I stopped myself before I placed any twenties on the counter.

"I'm sorry," I blurted out, expecting a swift smack across the face.

She might have liked to show off her goods, but she wasn't going to get pushed around when guys like me got fresh.

"I just got back into town from a long trip and I couldn't help myself. It's something I always wanted to do."

Maybe it was just that she liked to fuck celebrities or people who knew them. But she took off her apron.

"Juan," she called out to the back of the kitchen. "I have to go to the bank."

I stared into the kitchen where the tall, unshaven and emaciated looking short order cook, who had rings beneath his eyes, was peeling an onion.

I could see he had many irons in the fire, from the three different pans in which he was sautéing vegetables and chicken, together with the huge oven in which he baked their homemade tortillas.

As Nelsa threw her apron onto the top of a large black can of lard, a big plume of smoke filled the kitchen, momentarily making Juan look like the sorcerer's apprentice.

There was an awkward moment when we walked out of the restaurant together and Juan threw something out of the frying pan and into the fire, howling and cursing as he was hit by a spray of grease.

Nelsa looked back at me, then down at her watch. It was one of those gold imitation Rolexes that the Nigerian vendors hawk in Times Square. The time piece fit perfectly with her love of celebrities and glamour. It was like owning a pimp mobile.

You had to go out of the restaurant onto the street to enter my building. I nervously fumbled in my pocket to find my keys. It was a very narrow entranceway and vestibule. I was worried Nelsa's ass might not fit through. How was she going to negotiate the five flights of stairs tottering on her high platform heels?

I walked behind her, to break her fall. She wouldn't have been the first woman whose spiked heels got caught in those rickety stairs. I was awakened on several occasions by the cries of tumbling bodies. I remembered seeing a SUNY Downstate ambulance arrive. It had been a particularly egregious incident where an inebriated hottie fractured her coccyx.

Nelsa was humming the Buena Vista Social Club's "El Cuarto del Tula." I panted as I usually did on the steep climb. I wanted to touch her, but felt curiously inhibited. A lot of sex for me has always been about muscle memory. My first impulse as I fumbled anxiously for my keys, standing awkwardly in front of the black painted door to my apartment with its copper number 5, was to smack her in the face.

I also had the urge to give her a good swift kick in the butt and bend her over my knee just to let her know who was in charge. I learned these things about handling women from watching an animal trainer under the big top, as a kid when the traveling circus came to town. Pornhub videos solidified my education.

A little bit of knowledge is a dangerous thing. Now, the meetings tempered my urges. They removed all the exhilaration and glory of conquest. Even if she were compliant, you never knew what was going on someone's head. The thought of treating Nelsa like an animal was not turning me on.

In the absence of my usual fun and games, I found myself relying on small talk about the building and its state of disrepair. I stuck my tongue into her mouth as I kissed her in the restaurant, which was a start, but beyond trying to spout out the usual insults that didn't come, I didn't know what to say.

"Excuse the mess," I said, as I kicked a pair of jockey shorts and some smelly socks off my bed onto the floor. "I just got back from vacation."

"Did you go to Florida?"

"Camelot, I met King Arthur!" I was about to tell her about fucking Gwen, but I stopped myself, realizing that I was only bragging out of insecurity.

"Oh, so you were in Jersey."

"No, seventh century England."

"Yeah, my cousin does the medieval pageant thing in Bayonne where they got the suits of armor and joust. It's cool."

I wanted to pull out all the stops and really tell her that I had traveled a little farther than the Jersey shore, but it's almost impossible to describe wormholing to people who haven't hit "a bottom."

At first, we awkwardly sat next to each other on the sofa as I babbled about the apartment and its décor or lack thereof. Then when I timorously put my hand on her thigh as I was going on about how I disposed of my recyclables, she touched her finger to my lips, pulling me closer.

I thrust my tongue into her mouth again and whispered, "Oh baby, you're really hot."

I groped at her breasts like an adolescent and dug my fingers under the elastic waistband of her spandex pants—looking for underwear that didn't exist.

I was right about her being hot. Hot barely did justice to it. I would never be able to satisfy her.

I fiddled around like a gynecologist performing an exam. With my adrenalin spiking, my body started to shake as my nerves got the better of me.

On the school bus as a teenager, I always tried to hide the tent in my pants, but now it was turning into one of those circus disasters where the crowds panic as the big top starts to fall. Trying to repair a computer by turning it on and off repeatedly in the hope that the missing program will suddenly pop up, is more the idea. Finally, after looking at me quizzically as I continued my mechanical excavations of her reproductive system, she put her hand on my crotch. Her fingers danced around as if she were trying to catch a pest. Then she withdrew when she failed to find anything. Hoping to remedy the situation, she got up from the sofa and pulled her T-shirt over her head.

I felt like I already knew her breasts since she never wore a bra. But they turned out to be larger than I expected, with dark aureoles and oversized nipples. They were so imposing and direct that they looked like interrogators. Her tits were like a tanked-up guest at a dinner party.

I blamed her, just like I always did with women when I couldn't get it up. There was no way that I could accuse her of not being sexy enough. However, I still managed to do it, by convincing myself that she was being too aggressive. If she had been more subtle and seductive— even passive—then I would have been able to take over. If she wore a bra, I would at least have had to take it off. Revealing too much too soon killed the mystery. You don't get turned on when you go to a nude beach and everyone is already undressed. It was easy to rattle off all the excuses. I'd done it so many times before. If I didn't find something wrong with her then the blame was going to fall on my back.

Normally I would have fucked her tits and then her mouth, but too much was going on in my head, where the deconstructing was directly proportional to the shrinking of my dick. It was similar to getting one of those messages on your cell phone, *All circuits are being used. Please call back later.*

I could see the disappointment on her face when she reached down into my pants and found my limp rotted baby carrot.

I panicked and then fell into despair when I realized that nothing was going to happen.

You can't will an erection!

Jerry's words were like an alarm going off.

I fumbled and joylessly continued to finger her cunt. It remained intimidatingly wet. As she groaned both out of desire and frustration, I remembered Christ's words on the cross, "God, why has thou forsaken me?"

She got up and bent over to extricate her pants from the pile. Then I watched her wriggle back into them, making a little emphatic jump. She was obviously in a hurry. I got a second wind, as I peeked at her beautiful Hispanic bush disappearing into tight fitting fabric.

Then it was over. As Nelsa turned away, her beautiful ass rebuked me for the last time.

At meetings people always talked about starting the day over. I wondered if I could erase what happened, as you do with a cursor when you eliminate a sentence from a paragraph. Could Nelsa and I be actors in a rehearsal and replay the scene?

As she stood in front of me buttoning her jeans, she looked like a prisoner in some country famous for human rights abuses. In my desperate and futile attempt to excite myself, I replayed one of my favorite porn loops, "The Girl with the Bag Over Her Head." The plot is simple: a naked girl gives a blowjob through the hole in the paper bag that covers her head.

"I never thought you liked me," Nelsa said.

"It has nothing to do with you." I was surprised by my own honesty.

When she finished dressing, I walked over to her and held her face in my hands, but her body stiffened. Even though I had begun to feel turned on when she took off her T-shirt, something was stopping me. I felt her slinking away, a fish, fighting for its life as it tries to wriggle out of your hands. Her eyes welled up for minute. Then I could see the neighborhood coming out in her as she gave me a cold hard stare that told me to keep my distance.

Even though we were in my place, I'd become the intruder.

I went to take a leak. By the time I returned, she was gone. There was something almost jubilant about the sound of her heels, as she bounded down the stairs. They sounded like a pair of maracas.

When I went to look for her several hours later, under the guise of pretending I needed to get something to eat, she wasn't behind the counter.

"What can I get you buddy?" Juan said, sizing me up like I was some stranger who just moseyed in off the street.

Had she said anything? He had to know something was amiss.

"Is Nelsa around?" I said squeamishly, looking over his shoulder into the kitchen with a mixture of fear and hope that she would magically pop up out of nowhere.

He picked up the phone for a delivery order. I didn't wait for the response. I was still not getting it. I was putting the cart before the horse, in constantly fixating on my erections instead of who I was having them with. Did I really care about Nelsa, or was I simply disappointed that after all my travels, I still hadn't solved my problem?

Back in the Pliocene era, I had cared about someone, but I also had no worries getting it up. I thought that Nelsa was simply angry about not getting fucked, but could it be that she was annoyed that I was only interested in my dick and didn't show the least bit of concern for her or her feelings? I had been so ruffled by own performance that I didn't have the courtesy to attend to her needs. Why hadn't I gone down on her?

For a moment, I contemplated heading back to Camelot where, speaking of horses, I was a big shot—at least in the eyes of Gwen. It certainly was better than being a nobody. But I would really miss my cold Diet Cokes and the delicious burritos and quesadillas you got in the Downtown Cafe. Then there was the fact that my inhabiting Hank

Morgan back in the Middle Ages was just an act. Hank wasn't even real. He was just a character in fiction. And there was nobody I could really talk to about my problems in Camelot…no Jerry, no Wormhole Society.

18

Jerry

You always think that you will be missed at the meetings when you've been away, but I felt a little irritated that even Sonya and Tiffany didn't seem to notice my absence.

It was only when I realized that I HADN'T REALLY BEEN ANYWHERE as far as the others were concerned—and all my experiences occurred in a nanosecond— that I was able to calm down and listen to the speaker. It turned out to be Jerry, celebrating his twenty-fifth anniversary.

I hadn't seen him sitting in the audience bank. It was an eye opener to realize that he himself was on the roster.

They always say that *you're where you're supposed to be*. But Jerry was going to have some explaining to do. Why didn't he let on that he was one of us in the first place? I'd heard that many therapists and facilitators at Wormhole rehabs were also recovering Worms. However, they often retained their anonymity with patients. Jerry had struck me as very street, not someone who would hide behind a professional veneer.

Now of course I was hearing his story for the first time. It didn't involve ladyboys, services like Dial-A-Slave or places like the Bang Bang Club. He'd been a social worker who fell in love with clients who happened to be sex workers. His wife left him when she found out and he was fired from his job with the city.

All of this had happened back in a parallel universe that was still going on in the 1970s. His style of dress—gold chains, tight open shirts and platform shoes—were, I now realized, reminiscent of the disco era. Back then there was no Wormhole Society. His journey had taken to him to a future dimension where he was able to get help and help others too.

As Jerry talked, I kept trying to make eye contact with him. Either he didn't see me or was attempting to preserve his therapeutic neutrality.

It was at that point that I felt in my pocket and found a piece of bone. Knowing immediately what it was, I involuntarily cried out, "I'm going to be rich!"

On one of our outings, Lucy took me to a burial ground. She handed me the fossilized remains of what I took to be one of her ancestors. Even though there were really no words for birth or death in Australopithicanese, it turned out to be ironic, since her own remains would someday be the source of her fame.

Could we be living in one eternal present? For a moment I experienced a sense of longing for our life together. I wondered if this blatant disregard for the rules of space and time weren't her doing.

Primitive men and women may not have had our reasoning abilities. They were like animals in that they had intuitive abilities we didn't possess. Perhaps she had planted the bone on me as a means of reeling me back in, without really understanding the full implications of what she was doing.

For a moment I toyed with the idea of journeying back to the Pliocene era and attempting to bring her back with me.

"That monkey girl loved me," I mumbled.

This time an older woman sitting in front of me turned and sternly told me to "Shush!"

When I muttered "Fuck you," she growled threateningly

It was like the immigrants at the turn of the twentieth century. I remembered my grandfather telling me stories about how he had journeyed back to the old country to bring his lady to America.

I wondered what Lucy would look like when she made it into the present dimension. This also filled me with apprehension. The form she existed in when I knew her had become a skeleton, now exhibited at the Museum of Natural History. But what if, in some parallel universe, she was transformed? What if in some future dimension, she became a raving bitch?

After Jerry spoke, there was the usual secretary's break with its announcements of Wormhole events and anniversaries together with a collection of contributions. Then, the sharing began from the floor. I was a little hesitant to put my hand up, fearing that I would obsess if Jerry didn't call on me, but I couldn't help myself.

I should have known, there was nothing to worry about. "I'm Rusty and I'm a Worm."

"Hi Rusty," the others responded.

"I just want to check in and let everyone know that I just got back from the Middle Ages. It's nice to be home."

I walked up toward the crowd that surrounded Jerry at the end of the meeting, clutching tightly the little piece of bone which was no bigger than my thumb. I was sure he was going to slough me off. He was one of those people who managed to retain a certain degree of arrogance and ego despite supposedly working a spiritual program. But I decided to go through the motions.

When you start going to meetings, you learn the etiquette. One of the central elements is "act as if." Another is, "feelings aren't facts," a principle which was vindicated when waiting my turn to shake Jerry's hand, he pulled me aside and said, "I have to speak to you…right away. Can you hang around afterwards?"

I was sure I'd done something wrong. Had I abused my privileges? I had heard about "speeding," which was like drag racing through wormholes. Maybe I'd gone too far—into the past, that is. Maybe there were some prohibitions I didn't know about. Was journeying back to the beginning of time allowed?

There had always been a bit of bluster about Jerry. I began to realize that he probably was just being seductive and didn't really have anything to say. Just as I figured, it was all hype. When he finally came out of the church, he was accompanied by a hot looking chick in Goth attire. Only as an afterthought, he turned back to say, "You look great, kid."

A lot of people claim they really have to talk to you when they don't. He undoubtedly acted like this with everyone.

"I need to talk to you," I called out.

"You got my number."

"Yeah, I do," I bitterly thought.

I attempted to visualize the sandwich board in front of the Downtown Cafe. But I felt distracted by Jerry's hot and cold behavior. I suddenly was distrustful of everyone. It was lucky I had Lucy's bone, or I might have started to think it was all one big optical illusion or hallucination. Perhaps my whole life was a dream from which I had yet to awaken.

I wasn't sure what to do with a hot bone. I knew I had to get it carbon dated. My next stop was the Department of Paleontology at the Museum of Natural History. But how would I explain myself? That's one of the many problems with wormhole travel to parallel universes. You can't tell anybody where you've been. They're not going to understand, nor would they buy the idea that my discovery simply resulted from a hobby, i.e., looking for fossilized remains of extinct species.

The fact was, beyond recognizing Lucy as a scientific celebrity, I didn't know anything about paleontology. I knew as little about it as I did about the bosons and muons. I'd had rapid-fire conversations back at the Big Bang, that all concluded, *It doesn't matter.*

I decided to climb into a wormhole and head up to the diamond district on 47th Street. The trade in gems and jewels is handled by Orthodox Jews who know everything and would surely have suggestions about where I could unload a prehistoric bone.

His name was Shlomo Shapiro. He wore a yarmulke and had payes hanging on the sides of his face. They say everything is as meant to be and that there are no coincidences. I had a slight suspicion he was one of the men I had seen that first day in Jerry's office.

"Are you interested in parallel universes?"

Shlomo didn't respond, as he was still intently examining the bone through his eyepiece.

"It's very old, but we don't handle this kind of merchandise."

I suffer from OCD. Once I have started a line of inquiry, I find it hard to stop.

"You know the doctrine of eternal recurrence, the idea that over infinite time and space there will be not only a duplicate of the world we live in, but infinite variations where, say, the diamond district ends up on 48th rather than 47th Street?"

Shlomo turned away and rapidly spoke in Yiddish to his cohort at the next counter.

He pushed the bone towards me.

"Would you like a plastic bag?"

I was about to ask where else I might go with it, when he beckoned towards the next customer in line—a sleazy looking character wearing a tattered black leather jacket and knit hat who looked like he was trying to unload some hot items.

Should I have been more insistent? No pain, no gain. Sometimes you must be pushy. What if I had indeed seen Shlomo outside Jerry's office? What if he knew something that he was reluctant to reveal?

By the time I returned to my apartment, I felt there were still some loose ends.

It was already 4:30 and I noted that the gem store's hours were from 8:30 to 5. I could have climbed into another wormhole, but it almost seemed immoral when a half hour was involved. So I simply grabbed the F.

5:00 and 5:30 came, but no Shlomo. When he did leave, I almost missed him because of the fur shtreimel he now had on his head.

"You can't do this in public. It's heresy for us Satmars. God created the world in seven days and that was it."

With that Shlomo just stalked off, becoming indistinguishable as he disappeared into a sea of Chasidic Jews in their long black coats and fur hats. Since I was there when the heavens and the earth had been created, I could have told Shlomo a thing or two, but I was still too jet lagged to argue.

19

The Bone

My rent was due. All I had was a prehistoric bone. I'd talk about it at the meetings. Money wouldn't solve all my problems, even if I got lucky and made a sale. Also, there was the obvious association with the boner that I had to go back to the Pliocene era to attain. I still plainly wasn't comfortable in my own skin. In running back through recorded and unrecorded history I was doing what people in the program called "taking a geographic."

It was like *National Geographic* when I journeyed back to the Pliocene.

I had a great orgasm as a particle in the Big Bang. Who wouldn't? But was that how I wanted to spend my life? As a New Yorker I was already leading a hurried existence and the prospect of spending the rest of my years having one night (or nanosecond) stands with Holly Golightlys was a high price to pay.

I could have wormholed myself to the Museum of Natural History, but I decided to take the subway again, this time the B which would land me right on Central Park West. I had a hunch that this is what my facilitator Jerry would tell me, that I had to narrow the circle and concentrate on a finding a dimension of comfort that was closer to home. I would have gone right over to see him, if I weren't afraid he would rain on my parade. I had a hunch he would make light of my bone and not even get what it represented. One of the most disappointing things I discovered in all my travels through space and time is that most people don't listen.

I went right up to the foggy glass doors at the end of the long marble-floored corridor with its auspicious thirty-foot high ceilings from which hung ancient fluorescent lights. The Department of Paleontology was right next to the Department of Primatology. From the lower floors I could hear the recorded sounds of monkeys in a rain forest that greeted tourists who entered the galleries.

I was afraid I was going to have to fill in a whole bunch of forms the way you do on intake in a doctor's office or hospital. But there was just a young woman manning the little reception desk as she studied a textbook. I informed her I had a specimen I thought might be promising and needed to be examined. She told me to wait and disappeared behind another set of swinging mahogany doors, with the number 404 embossed in chipped gold lettering.

"I'm a friend of Lucy's," was the first thing I said, parroting the old AA catchphrase, being "a friend of Bill's."

"Oh, she's right in that case down the hall."

The paleontologist reminded me of John Kenneth Galbraith. He was tall and stooped, with an overly large head, and wore a threadbare jacket that was too small. He never could have dreamt that I wasn't joking about Lucy.

"It actually looks like a large toenail, probably of an amphibian. Could be a tortoise."

He raised the small magnifying glass hanging from a lanyard on his neck, fitting it right into his eye socket. He was one of those itinerant researchers who treat people just as they do bees or ants in a colony. He was a computer printout of the absent-minded professor and appeared to be almost indiscriminate when it came to data collection. He was already classifying me along with my bone.

I was waiting for him to ask where I'd found the bone. Naturally, I couldn't tell him the truth. When he didn't ask and simply continued to stare between the object and me, I thought maybe he understood. Who knew? Perhaps he was one of those scholars gifted with preternatural abilities exceeding the limits of science. The people in the program are always saying there are no coincidences.

"I found it in Central Park, near Strawberry Fields," I lied, as he held the bone up to the light. I have a hunch it might be something important."

"Yeah, we should probably carbon date it," he said, skeptically, handing it back to me.

He looked surprised when I nervously grabbed the bone back as he put it back down on the table.

"Is some kind of reward offered when someone brings in something like this?"

"Generally, a fossilized remain is the property of the country in which it's been discovered. I don't remember any of the major finds being scrutinized for their commercial potential. But I'm sure it happens. Just about everything ends up being monetized, don't you think? That's the nature of modern life. Why don't you leave it here overnight. I'll run some scans and try to figure out where it's from."

"No thanks."

He looked surprised.

Passing through the doors, I broke into a run. I had no idea what he was after, but I wasn't about to take any chances. Maybe he was right. Maybe the bone wasn't worth anything, but I wasn't in a trusting mood. The moment I got out on the street, I simply visualized the Downtown Cafe sign and found myself standing right back in front of my building.

I knew the wall-eyed fellow behind the counter at the newsstand up the block was a fence. Those guys are only after jewelry and Rolex watches. He wouldn't go for a prehistoric bone. And now I wasn't even sure I wanted to relinquish this artifact of my relationship with Lucy.

I held on to it tightly, kneading it in my hand as if it were a magical amulet. I still hadn't found what I was looking for. In the program they always warn you not to give up before the miracle, but after all my travels I still hadn't gotten anywhere. Sure, I could get an erection in the Stone Age. Yet what about the real me? Every time I passed the Bang Bang Club, I was still tempted. Fortunately, I realized that it was unlikely I was going to find the solution to my problems by hooking up with people who were even more desperate than I was. I had no choice but to stay the course.

I thought about Tiffany and Sonya, back when everyone went to the diner after the meetings. These trips into the past were now complicating my life more than helping. I didn't really need to travel back 3.2 million or even 1,100 years to get hard. Even if the whole idea of wormholing was that you could find your better self in some parallel universe, I was missing the whole part of the program that had to do with helping other people. Some problems were just unshakeable. Maybe I would never find that better self who treated women and ladyboys like human beings, and didn't have to worry about getting it up all the time.

As I headed towards the church, I saw a pile of chicken bones sitting on a discarded KFC tub. On an impulse, I took my bone out of my pocket and tossed it in with the other garbage. Was this what it meant to surrender? Was this what it was to turn your will and life over to a higher power?

"Welcome to Time Travelers." Every meeting has its soubriquet. This one felt particularly pertinent for me now.

The room had been filled with jabber and grew suddenly quiet. Tiffany, the chairperson, sat next to Sonya, who was secretary.

"My name is Tiffany and I'm a Worm. Worms meet here in the church of the Earthly Resurrection on Mondays and Thursdays at 6:30. We have a beginners meeting on Tuesdays and Thursdays at 12:30. We celebrate anniversaries on the last Monday of every month. If you are interested in celebrating with us, please inform the chairman at the beginning of the meeting. I've asked Phil to read the preamble."

"I'm Phil and I'm a Worm."

"Hi Phil," the group replied in a chorus. "The Wormhole Society is a twelve-step recovery program based on the principles of Alcoholics Anonymous. We are not aligned with any politics, sect or religion, neither endorses nor opposes any causes. We aim to achieve sobriety by placing our body into dimensions which remove us from our most self-destructive tendencies. Our primary purpose is to stay sober and help other Worms to achieve sobriety."

"Our speaker had to cancel at the last minute," Tiffany continued. "So, is there anyone who would like to share their experience, strength and hope with the group?"

Like a person with Tourette Syndrome who can't control their mouth, my hand rose involuntarily. The group was clapping for me before I could say no.

"I'm very pleased to introduce Rusty, a member of our group who will qualify for fifteen minutes, after which we'll have a secretary's break followed by a round robin until 5:10 and then a show of hands."

"I'm Rusty." For a moment I paused…not quite sure if I were ready to describe myself as others had done at meetings. I looked towards Sonya who gave me the nod I needed to proceed.

"And I'm a Worm. I definitely qualify to be a member of this program. I was brought up in one of those families in which everything was safe and secure, but where there was nothing to live for. My mother didn't like to touch or be touched. She rarely hugged or kissed you. But food was always on the table which sat in front of a television. Instead of talking, we were glued to the TV all through dinner. The bleakest periods of my childhood occurred when the television was broken. We just sat there. My father didn't like the Russians. He thought we should bomb them before they bombed us, even if it meant that Armageddon would be the result. He frequently warned me not to let myself get sucker punched. My mother didn't care much about politics.

"Supper was the usual spaghetti and meat sauce and buttered bread, or it could be, say, a Hungry Man Fried Chicken TV dinner or beans and franks—standard fare. The only unusual thing from childhood, and it was something that only came back to me when I started to go to meetings, was that my older brother made me dress up like a girl. He told me he needed practice and fondled me. Once he even made me bleed when he tried to fuck me in the ass. He also put his prick in my mouth, telling me that this is what girls would do for me with their mouths when I got older. I really didn't think much of it at the time."

I stopped talking when I heard someone snapping their fingers—a sign they were being triggered by my explicit remembrances.

"Sorry I'll try to be a little less graphic," I said. "I'm just accounting for the way I am, but at this stage in my recovery all the pieces of the puzzle are not exactly fitting into place. There's a big black hole that occurs during adolescence…and speaking of black holes…."

I was about to tell them about the Big Bang and the Bang Bang Club, but I realized that it might be best if I stuck to the basics. I'd tell Tiffany and Sonya all about my travels over coffee at the diner.

"I don't even remember very much about my first sexual relationship. It had nothing to do with what people call lovemaking. There was no kissing or affection. I didn't fall for someone like most adolescents. I met an older woman online and it set a pattern in which I produced certain cocktails of behavior that either turned me on or didn't. I didn't become a Worm because I wanted to be a better person."

A hand shot up, indicating I was again triggering someone. Sonya looked exasperated.

"I guess, I've said enough, I'll leave it at that."

There was a surprised silence and then perfunctory applause that was a bit lighter than what occurs after someone tells their story at your average Wormhole meeting.

"Thank you, Rusty," Sonya intoned, as I sat back in my seat. "We have no dues or fees, but we do have expenses. So please give if you can. If you can't, just keep coming back. We need you more than your money."

After the collection and announcement, there was a short break. Strangers obligatorily came over, one after the other, to shake my hand and tell me to keep coming, which I knew was a euphemism for telling me I didn't know anything. When the secretary called the meeting back to order, I picked on Tiffany to start the round robin.

"Thanks Rusty," she said. "That was really a terrific first qualification. I remember back to when I first came into the program. I was so mocus I didn't know whether I was coming or going. I personally enjoyed your honesty. I'm feeling a little bit shaky today. I have been dating this really cool girl. She has everything I thought I was looking for, but I'm not in love."

She paused. I could see her eyes were welling up.

"What is love, throwing yourself at the feet of someone who abuses you and then rejects you? I just have never understood what having a relationship is all about. I guess I'm still looking for the cheap thrill that comes from lusting after someone or something that isn't there. Anyway, congratulations Rusty. I got a lot out of what you said. I've enjoyed getting to know you over coffee at the diner."

Sonya was next. I was so nervous I actually pissed my pants a little. She smiled before she started to speak, but then her expression changed. Her lips trembled and her hazel eyes pierced right through me. I had once seen the testimony of a rape victim in one of those Truth and Reconciliation Commissions that were established in the wake of the atrocities in Tunisia. That barely repressed desire for retribution was what I saw on her face. I had paid for her services, but I'd also been one of her torturers.

"I'm Sonya and I'm a Worm."

"Hi Sonya."

There was even something strange about the chorus. I felt everyone knew.

"Thanks Rusty. This is obviously a very special moment for you and a painful one for me—since we knew each other in our old lives and are an important part of each other's qualification."

My fingers, which had been gently rapping across the table at which I sat, now gripped the sides of my metal foldout chair. I had to stop myself from rushing out of the room in shame. It was one thing to reveal all the intimate details of your life in front of the group. There was even a thrill in producing a shock effect and testing the frequently repeated notion of "let us love you until you love yourself." But it was another when someone was doing the talking for you. Would people really love a guy whose story involved violence and was even criminal in its tales of degrading sex which violated human dignity? Who was going to love a person whose fantasied destruction of women and ladyboys was the only way he could get off?

I felt defensive even before she started since underneath it all I still felt Sonya was just a whore. I'd already paid for what I done. I was just another John who frequented hot spots like the Bang Bang Club and even the Big Bang when he was looking for kicks.

"I have to be honest," she continued. "When I saw you that first day you came in, I felt sick to my stomach. And it was this wonderful program that enabled me to see you as a suffering Worm rather than just hating you for the way you were.

When I was out there, I suffered from the Stockholm Syndrome. The more you tortured me, the more I loved you. Denial was definitely a river in Egypt in my case. I rationalized my feelings by thinking you were a poor sick person, an abandoned dog or cat, I was going to save.

"During those days, I actually worked for the Animal Rescue League. It was the only thing that made me feel good about myself, after all the nights of unspeakable degradations I endured from clients like you. But I have to also say, you were different. You weren't kidding yourself, like so many of the others. You didn't pretend you were being something you weren't. You weren't the kind of John who kisses sweetly and then administers a brutal slap in the face. I have plenty of scars to show from those kinds of guys. You made no excuses. You had a no-holds-barred attitude. That time you threw me to the ground, shoved me out the front door naked and dumped all the bills on top of my naked body was the closest thing I had ever felt to love, believe it or not. As I lay totally naked on the floor outside your door with only money to cover my shame, I finally reached my bottom.

"The next day I attended my first Wormhole meeting. Since then, I have begun to live a life beyond my wildest dreams. Who would have ever thought that a submissive prostitute, who had so little self-esteem that she felt flattered to be kicked around like a stray dog, would one day be traveling all through the multiverse in search of both a new exo- and endoskeleton? And who would have thought I would ever have had access to words like that?"

Fingers snapped wildly in response to Sonya's triggering language, but Tiffany pretended not to see them.

"You did me a favor by telling me I was no better than a piece of shit. If you weren't what you were back then, I would never have had the opportunity to become the person I was meant to be."

I didn't hear any of the other shares. I was shaken and totally humiliated by Sonya. I felt like I'd been mugged by both her and Tiffany who, under the guise of honesty, had hit me below the belt and blown my anonymity by making my amends for me.

I had been persuaded by Jerry and others in the program that I was suffering from a disease. I wasn't a bad person. I was just a sick person trying to get better. However, Sonya was painting me as an evil and immoral person—who she was now punishing with public humiliation. I had the feeling that if she could, she would have had me arrested for my crimes.

Hardly anybody came up to me afterwards; there was none of the obligatory backslapping and praise for my courage. It felt like the combination of my and Sonya's willingness to speak our minds had resulted in my exile from God's grace and from the love of the other members. Naturally any of the secret hopes I'd harbored about working through my problems and having a real relationship with Sonya were down the tubes.

I hated myself and felt perilously close to having a slip in which I'd call Dial-a-Slave. I needed some relief. Hurting others and undoing all the work I'd done on myself had been my usual solution in the past. It was an invidious cycle in which I punished myself for things I was ashamed of, always upping the ante to insure further punishment.

Now I was even an outcast among my own people, the ones who had promised to love me until I loved myself. I was removed from the category of sick people trying to get better to that of simply a bad person, an exploiter, a sexual predator who was no better than Eichmann, Hitler or Goebbels—unless you took the attitude that they too were sick and needed to join a program for recovering tyrants. I was beginning to laugh to myself imagining Hitler's qualification, "and then I took the Sudetenland and marched into Poland, but it still wasn't enough."

What was I laughing about? It wasn't funny. I could go to another meeting where I wasn't known, but rumors spread. I was paranoid as it was. I had nowhere to go.

I was filled with sadness. It wasn't an emotion I knew much about. The last time I cried was in elementary school. On my final day of sixth grade, my supposed friends had passed me over when they were picking up sides for punch ball. I came home teary-eyed, but my mother wasn't sympathetic. Now, I was experiencing the same sense of dejection. My supposed friends had shown their real colors. The only reason Tiffany had encouraged me was to out me in front of the group.

At the very moment I was deep in these thoughts, I felt a hand touching my elbow. I figured it was one of the weirdos who came to meetings, not to stay sober, but to find partners to act out with.

I was shocked when I saw *her*.

She was one of those people whose eyes water before they even utter a word. I immediately felt embarrassed by her display of emotion. Anger was a trigger in and of itself, since it's the only emotion I ever experienced in my lousy sex life, except when I'd gone back to my prehistoric self in the Pliocene era or when I'd become one of the first particles back at the Big Bang. I didn't count my fling with Gwen, since it was a case of *noblesse oblige* that happened so quickly that I didn't have time to have any feelings at all.

For a moment I was dumbstruck, not knowing how to take her touching me. Was it a gesture of reconciliation, a come-on or even a slip? Would she punish herself for her candor, unleashing emotions that I would then have to leash—by putting a collar around her neck?

Then again, maybe she wasn't done telling me off. Behind the veneer of vulnerability was a prosecutor. I was afraid that under the guise of apologizing for hanging me in public, she would lure me to another interrogation. I could see myself sitting before Tiffany and her in the diner and facing their cold hard stares.

My first impulse was to head right back to Camelot where I could at least claim I was a big shot, and where I could also say I was not as fucked up as Gwen in the acting out department. At least, I hadn't forced myself on a horse or other barnyard animal.

I promised myself I would just listen.

However, when she warned me "you're on a death trip" I got angry. What right did she have to tell me that?

I bolted.

My eyes met Sonya's through the window of the diner, as I walked back home.

20

Flatlining

When I called Jerry's office to make an appointment, there was a new answering machine message which gave four prompts: *Press #1 if you are a doctor or caregiver, press #2 if you are a patient, press #3 if this is an emergency, press #4 to schedule or confirm an appointment.*

The message didn't sound at all like Jerry, whose brash borscht belt irascibility and humor were always part of the spiel.

Most of the people who passed through were seen on a pro bono basis and I'd heard that the basic way Jerry made money was through the Wormhole retreats, which took place at a host of rehabs with names like Alternate Universes or Multiversity.

Now that I knew he was one of us, I was afraid he might have slipped himself. It's hard when someone you respect and look up to as a power of example goes off the wagon. However, now, as I felt how fragile my connections with Tiffany, Sonya and Jerry were and how easy it was to fall out of the loop, I drew upon one of the simplest adages of the program, *A day at a time*. I just had to get through the day.

When you're looking for a miracle that will spare you from your current problems, the cupboard is always empty. I didn't even bother to look into the Downtown Cafe to see if Nelsa was back. By the time I climbed the five flights to my place, I was exhausted and out of breath. I lay down on my couch and fell into a deep sleep. I dreamt about the sandwich board downstairs and immediately was wafted away.

I found myself inside Nelson Rockefeller's elegant 54th Street townhouse. A body undulated under me. I could feel the garters and stockinged legs of my lover, who was splayed on the bed. I felt her wetness as I tasted her lips. Then my chest was constricted by searing pain. The soreness remained with me as my eyes flashed to a menu from the restaurant of the Dorset Hotel down the street. The menu recalled the sandwich board, which wafted me back to the present. I was still experiencing a shortness of breath. It was like one of those dreams of falling. Even though I awakened, I still felt dizzy.

I had tried masturbating with a rope tied around my neck before, but now I found myself awakening in David Carradine's Bangkok hotel room, gagging to death as the chair slipped from under me. I was left trapped in the mixture of asphyxiation and orgasm resulting from my garrote.

They say that in your last moments, your whole life flashes in front of you. What better lesson could I have learned in finding a pleasure so mind-blowingly intense—in this ultimate come—that I almost didn't escape from? Now it was clearer to me than ever that all my search for hard-ons and pleasure masked the desire to destroy myself and anyone who was unfortunate enough to get in my way.

I was only spared when I looked out the window of my Soi Cowboy hotel to see a flashing neon sign advertising Tex-Mex, food, tortillas, quesadillas. Again, one thing led to the next and I was enabled to envision the sandwich board just in the nick of time.

And then I was in the boudoir of the newly wedded Attila the Hun. I felt a sharp pain as I tore away the hijab that covered my betrothed face, seeking her lips. I was only spared by the sight of the table of delicacies, which included a finely shaped mound of rice—something which enabled me to bring up arroz y frijoles at the Downtown.

Could I have abused wormholing just like I did everything else in life? Were snafus popping up in the system due to misuse or overuse of certain functions?

It was like one of those accounts of a plane that's out of control and making a wild descent. I'd already had a couple of close calls. I was plainly in danger of crashing and burning at some place in history. Just when I started to relax thinking the roller coaster ride had come to an end, I made a brief stop at the deathbed of Errol Flynn, who died in the arms of his teenaged girlfriend, Beverly Aadland. I escaped by the skin of my teeth.

Poof. I was back in the present, still short of breath and with a lingering pain in my chest inherited from the alternate self that had almost died *in flagrante*. Nothing like this had ever happened before. I was defying all the rules of the multiverse.

I was terrified, realizing that I wasn't safe anywhere.

I thought of Cliff, my wormhole therapist over at the YMCA. Who knew where I would fly if I even glanced at the sandwich board on my way over to 19th and Broadway? My feeling about climbing into a wormhole, which is what I would normally have done if I wanted to get somewhere in an emergency, was similar to the apprehension of descending into the New York City subway system soon after 9/11.

I had to stay awake at all costs and not drift into another daydream that could be my undoing. I tried the meditating I learned about at a meeting, where you kept dirty thoughts at bay by counting breaths.

I found myself going down with the Titanic as the ship's musicians played "Nearer, My God, to Thee."

Throwing caution to the wind, I headed out to the street. It was the middle of the night. The Downtown Cafe was closed, with the sandwich board locked inside. Despite all the drunks, junkies and petty thieves lurking in the shadows, I felt momentarily safe. I wasn't going to fly off into history with a stampede of headlights coming at me as I crossed First Avenue.

Think back on your exercises, I told myself. If I could somehow replay the postures Cliff had taught me, I would be less likely to find myself being gassed, burned at the stake or waterboarded at some other moment in history.

Luckily, I had yet to find myself both "terminated with extreme prejudice" and "extraordinarily rendered" by the CIA. After all the near misses I'd already had, being a terrorist put to death was something I still had to look forward to. If I sucked my abs in, relaxed my shoulders, kept my back flat and my hips pushed forward, it would be easier to navigate myself through time on those occasions when I was inadvertently plucked out of the present.

I had no idea what was going on, but I had a hunch that my previous tripping had turned my space/time trajectory into the equivalent of a piece of Swiss cheese. I had dug my own grave by entering so many holes. Was my unconscious trying to tell me something? Was I continually tempting fate? Was I courting death under the guise of looking for a hot fuck? I'd almost been killed but managed to live. Had I finally learned my lesson?

When you're carousing late at night on the Lower East Side, you run into winos turned into self-appointed prophets. There are plenty of people who would nod sagely at an outlandish story which included travels to Camelot. Hell, half of the people on ecstasy or PCP have stories like my own. Yet I was in no mood to risk going up to my apartment in the middle of the night, where my dreams were likely to provide the fodder for further roller coaster rides. I remembered an old adage I'd heard at the meetings: "A worm in his own head is in enemy territory."

It wasn't the kind of white light experience that others at the meeting had talked about. However, as I was walking up First Avenue in the wee hours of the morning toward the darkened McDonald's, one of the numerous panhandlers with one leg, who was always aggressively working the avenue in his wheelchair asked for a buck. What almost stopped me in my tracks was that it was like seeing my reflection in a storefront window. He was me.

I'm the one with the problems is the attitude I usually have. Why should I do anything for him? I caught up with the wheelchair.

"Here." I held out a buck.

He grabbed it, like a squirrel secreting away a nut, without so much as a thank you. Then realizing that my unemployment checks would only go so far, I began to limit my giving to quarters, nickels and dimes. Still, I was laughing with a mixture of exhilaration and relief as I got rid of my change. If I gave it all away, I'd still be taken care of. The generosity of the multiverse was like warm sunlight. I instinctively knew I would no longer end up in a gas chamber, crematorium or hanging from the gallows. Both the impulse and the consequent fear had been lifted.

I should have thanked Sonya for upbraiding me, even if it did go against the principles of the fellowship. Indeed, I could have been arrested for some of the things I did if she had decided to press charges.

The only money left in my pocket was a $20 bill. I went into a twenty-four-hour Korean market on 7th and started to buy little bags of pretzels, nuts and crackers, along with some bottles of water. I took the plastic bag filled with snacks back along the avenue and passed them out whenever one of the homeless people lying in the gutter held out a hand.

I realized, as embarrassed as I was about what Sonya had said at the meeting, I had to go back so that I could reach out to another Worm who suffered as I had. It was precisely my experiences, however ugly they were, which would be of help to others encountering the same problems. I wasn't going to the meeting or descending into wormholes to get hard-ons. That had been my mistake. It was all in the preamble of the Wormhole Society: "My primary purpose is to stay sober and help other Worms to reach sobriety." My problem was that I never thought about anyone else but myself.

21

The Marquis

My near brushes with the guillotine and the gas chamber had changed me. I could still almost feel the blade, which had tickled as it touched my neck. Now I had a new perspective on life. Most importantly, I wasn't even obsessing on whether I got erections or not.

I'd think "Sonya" and then immediately put her out of my mind.

Nelsa had returned, but she was only working part-time since she was training to be a dental hygienist. I didn't know how to relate to her. I had no frame of reference. It would only happen if it was supposed to. At least that was the mantra I was practicing. *Everything was as it was supposed to be, or it would be different* was the expression.

I made an appointment with Cliff. Instead of abusing the wormhole by using it to avoid having to pay for the subway, I simply walked over to my sessions like a regular person. When I arrived at the basement rehab area, I cautiously approached a tall clean-shaven trainer with a Marine Corps-style buzz cut and said, "I'm looking for Cliff Rastafarian."

"Glad to meet you," he said reaching out his hand.

Shed of all the dreadlocks, Cliff looked much younger. In fact, he seemed like a vulnerable, teenaged boy.

I wasn't sure if he even recognized me. I was just another one of those clients who come once or twice then disappear.

He had me walk back and forth across the studio. Then he demonstrated the flying exercise that was exactly what he'd done on that first day when we met, months before. It was as if I were a new recruit. He was on auto-pilot.

I became afraid that he had also run into some "weather" as they say in the airline business. He was no longer the Cliff I originally knew. Maybe the new haircut was just the tip of the iceberg.

I quickly brought up the sign and within a flash found myself standing before the Cliff I knew and loved, dreadlocks and all. I had apparently mistakenly drifted into another dimension in which he'd attended some kind of therapeutic community, where they confronted inner problems with military-style discipline.

For a moment I was worried. Then I saw he recognized me. I brought up my sign, while he visualized his portal, and before long we were both taking a little cruise through the entrance to our respective wormholes. It was similar to skimming across the upper reaches of the atmosphere, right at the point where you depart from the gravitational pull of earth.

When I told him what had happened when I first showed up, he wasn't surprised. Apparently, despite all the rules of nondisclosure between universes, several other clients had met that version of him when they circled the present. It was an occupational hazard that went with the territory. Now that we were back in the right dimension, I was learning all kinds of new exercises, modeled on karate katas, the choreographed movements against an imaginary opponent.

Cliff explained that katas were useful since they told stories of perseverance amidst obstacles. There was one called Kanku, or "rising sun," that began with two hands meeting over the head that rendered the feeling of a new day beginning. It was perfect for Worms who had to struggle against their compulsions while enduring the dangers of time travel.

In the course of our hour together, Cliff also pulled the rug out from under me when he told me that Jerry had retired, without telling anyone where he'd gone.

"You'd essentially have to navigate the infinity of space and time to find him, which is not a very sober thing to do," he explained.

I was sad. Jerry meant a lot more to me than I did to him, which I guess was part of the grief I suddenly found myself contending with.

I was surprised at the dream I had after getting home from what had seemed a particularly productive session. It was a horrifying reliving of fucking Juanita up the ass in the dumpster, followed by the night I locked Sonya out of my apartment and threw the bills on her naked body. Only in this dream, Sonya was begging me to let her back in. I must have been screaming in my sleep since I woke up sweating and with my heart pounding. A child was crying. I soon found myself reassuring my downstairs neighbor who knocked on my door.

Plainly, as hard as I tried, I couldn't free myself from thoughts of Sonya. I was filled with such longing and guilt that I contemplated a kind of falling that had less to do with wormholes than the event horizons of black holes. It was fortunate that I had long ago misplaced the key for the fire escape's locked expansion security gate.

I knew I had to hightail it back to a meeting. It was the middle of the night. I would have to wait all the next day for the 5:30. But I had a plan, as the expression goes. My COBRA covered two more Wormhole therapy sessions, and I could always hang out in the diner. There were always program people there. Besides the Wormhole Society, AA, DA, OA and SA groups met there after their meetings. At least I'd feel safe. I made it through the day by hanging out at the Downtown Cafe, killing a few hours by watching daytime soaps and Oprah.

I was sure I'd see Tiffany and Sonya, but it was a small meeting. I didn't recognize hardly anyone which, considering my last go-round, made me feel comfortable again. Nevertheless, when it was over, I casually asked the tall balding fellow sitting next to me if Tiffany was still chairing.

He looked into my eyes.

"I heard that she and Sonya went out!"

It was like passing a crash on the highway. There was this lurid interest to know more. Even worse, I momentarily titillated myself with the temptation to call Dial-A-Slave under a pseudonym and ask if Sonya was back on the job.

I was reminded of *Candide*'s, "All's for the best in the best of all possible worlds." Only this was "All for the worst in the worst of all possible worlds." People apparently came and went at the meetings. It was unlikely anyone even remembered my qualification the other day. So, my fears of ostracism were unmerited. I realized it was a slippery slope. I could easily get into big-time trouble if I gave into the little thrill I was now experiencing in imagining what would happen if I were to throw caution to the wind.

I meditated and cleared my mind. But as the meeting started, I couldn't stop thinking of all the degrading acts I would make Sonya perform.

One of the many good things about wormholing is that it's a great way of preventing acting out. Instead of heading for the Bang Bang Club, I could go straight back to the Big Bang.

Someone who identified himself as "Joe" spoke next. Though I hadn't heard him before, he looked vaguely familiar. His hair was pulled back in a ponytail that gave it the look of one of those wigs worn by French aristocrats in the eighteenth century.

He told a story that was very similar to mine, without anyone snapping their fingers to indicate they were being triggered. He was a gagger. He liked to deep throat his whores to the point where they *gagged*.

"And I left them with a frosty beard," he laughed.

He loved having his way with desperate whores. Finally, he got sick and tired of using his penis as a tongue depressor.

I couldn't understand why no hands were going up, but I could see there definitely was a different complexion to this meeting. Later I learned it comprised a famously no-holds-barred group from St. Catherine's that was using our Earthly Resurrection space.

After Joe finished, they had the usual secretary's break with the seventh tradition collection. Newcomers, people working on ninety days and those celebrating a year or more of Wormhole sobriety, raised their hands. Then the sharing went to a round robin. I don't know whether Joe recognized a like-minded individual or if it was all pure chance. Instead of starting with the fetching young woman who had been crossing her legs provocatively in the front, he pointed to the very last seat in the back, where I was sitting. I was startled at first, but I had intended to raise my hand anyway due to how much I identified with his qualification. So, I wasn't at a loss for words.

"Hi Joe, thanks for your sharing. I really appreciated your honesty."

"Really?" he interrupted, looking seriously aroused.

"Actually, let me take that back. I hate it when people say that. I appreciated your courage in not mincing your words. My problem is that I get turned on by all the acting out. I still romanticize golden showers, facials, cock rings and clamps. I still like using clothes pins on a submissive. I like to make them hold their hands up like paws and bark like dogs."

Joe's nods and smiles of identification made me feel more at home than I'd ever been before. Maybe the members of this new group really told it like it was. The others who took offense and liked to talk vaguely about God and being in outer space could go elsewhere.

Even if there were those who objected to the candid way in which I was expressing myself, I felt strengthened by Joe's presence. He had a charisma and confidence that no one seemed to question. When I was done sharing, I didn't need to run for the hills. Though I'd dropped my load, my face wasn't hot with shame. When the meeting was over, one young woman even came up to me and told me how much she enjoyed my share.

Joe was short and slightly built with graying hair. He could have played a life insurance salesman in a television spot. He was surrounded by the usual crowd of glad-handers. I thought he would treat me as someone special due to the affinity I felt for him, but apparently the feeling wasn't mutual. Sometimes people felt you were stealing their thunder when you literally #metooed. He was surprisingly brusque when he got to me.

I tapped him on the shoulder just as he turned away to talk to someone else and asked for his number.

I told Cliff about Joe during our next session.

"Kind of silent type who looks normal," Cliff remarked. "Then he pops out with all this incredible stuff."

"I almost didn't believe him," I said. "I mean, the words didn't fit with the person who was saying them."

"He's been around a long time. He used to come here. I think he's an immigrant from another dimension of space and time. He's definitely not the Joe who did all that stuff."

At that moment it hit me. I didn't need to be a boson in the Big Bang or become a Neanderthal or a Connecticut Yankee in King Arthur's court. I just wanted to be your average Joe.

"I remember him referring to Lacoste. That was the Marquis de Sade's ancestral home," Cliff continued.

"You're shitting me."

"No, dude."

Far out, I thought. The Marquis de Sade will be my sponsor.

22

Therapy

I was having dreams in which I found myself at the Bang Bang Club being enticed by the sight of Sonya and Tiffany in the stocks, the devices they used as punishments in Puritan New England. What used to be enticing—for instance a room where naked bodies were hung upside down like sides of beef— was now the substance of nightmares from which I woke bathed in sweat. Then there were the dreams where they were tarred and feathered.

Of course, what I feared most was finding Sonya, her eyes dilated and willing to do anything I wanted, so long as I was willing to pay.

I get up early now to begin my job hunt, instead of coming home when everyone is going to work and then sleeping all day. I was relieved to find I was only dreaming. I thought of Joe as the Marquis and, one morning after a particularly fitful sleep, I called his number.

I knew I was contacting him to find comfort in hearing his VM message. The last thing I wanted was to really have to put my cards on the table. If I were looking for excuses, I could just say that I tried to reach out, but no one was there.

I was disconcerted when he picked up.

There was a pause after I identified myself as "Rusty from the meeting." I was sure he didn't remember me. Some people are great in front of crowds, but don't relate on a one-to-one a basis. If he were the reincarnation of the Marquis de Sade, he would be an exhibitionist who was better at getting attention than giving it. Well, at the very least I'd get him to autograph my copy of *The 120 Days of Sodom*. That was my personal Baedeker of depravity.

"I just wanted to check in and tell you how much I enjoyed your qualification the other day."

"Actually, my super is here with Con Ed," he replied. "I think there's a gas leak or something."

"No problem, I'll give you a buzz tomorrow."

I was sure I wasn't going to call back. I had enough trouble dialing his number in the first place, but when the next day rolled around and I still felt a severe urge to call Dial-A-Slave and/or look for Sonya at the Bang Bang Club, I figured I had nothing to lose.

This time there was no hesitation when I spoke my name. He knew who I was right away.

Joe was a good listener. I told him I had read *The 120 Days of Sodom*.

"I hope it was helpful," he remarked. There must have been a twinkle in his eye.

I knew from his talk that he was an old timer who'd been around the program for centuries. He had been an aristocrat in his past life and still was one to the extent that he was a veteran Worm.

He was a little like Bill W. and Doctor Bob, the founders of AA. It still felt good knowing someone who had flagellated servant girls and was now considered a well-respected member of the community. Nothing I did rivaled his exploits.

If he could completely change his life, then I certainly could take a wormhole to a dimension where I would finally be a regular Joe too.

My only problem was that I knew Sonya was out turning tricks and I was still holding on to the fantasy I could save her.

I was getting into a little routine. It was something I never had in my life which, even when it came to descending into wormholes, was always a matter of acting on impulse. In the morning I went down to the Downtown Cafe for my café con leche. Nelsa was working weekends. Our unpleasant little interlude might as well have never happened.

Under Cliff's guidance my wormholing totally changed—it was superficial and stuck closer to the surface. For instance, I tried parallel universes where things worked out with Muriel, Nelsa and even Sonya just to see what falling in love was all about.

When you get the gist, wormholing is a little bit like flying a plane. I was learning about my takeoffs and landings and working on touching down gently when coming off a turbulent flight. My galivanting randomly around the Big Bang and the Pliocene era was a little bit like going over Niagara Falls in a barrel. I was lucky I came out alive.

When you've become a real Worm, you navigate along the edges of your being. You don't attend Worm meetings to learn how to glide through the clear days when you have great visibility, you come to deal with those cloudy ones, the equivalent of bad weather on a psychic level.

I was dancing around the multiverse with such abandon that I almost got into some dangerous situations again, but an experienced Worm will deal with unstable conditions by deftly pulling into a nearby parallel universe where he can be himself on a nice day. People in AA were always intoning "Happiness is an inside job." Cliff liked to say, "it's an outside job" and counterintuitive. A true Worm learned to put old wine in new bottles, rather than new wine in old bottles. Amongst other things, wormholing turned adages upside down.

One day after I had lunch at the Downtown Cafe, Cliff accompanied me into a wormhole. This was a first since I thought you could only fly solo into parallel universes. He didn't want to go to any exotic locales. I mentioned South Beach. Cliff laughed off my idea, suggesting we just hang around the neighborhood—which ended up meaning that we were cruising very close to our own space/time coordinates. We went to a place where I got called in for an interview based on one of my responses to a position for an advertising salesman, and another in which Nelsa was talking to me about teeth.

Then, before I was trapped by unexciting dead-end existences, he got me right back to the limbo where I seemed comfortable, even though I wasn't getting closer to achieving any of my goals in regard to love or work. When you're flying so close to home, it's almost like you're not going anywhere; on the other hand, it takes a lot of skill. I could never have done it when I first started to wormhole. It's very easy to climb into a one and take off for an eternity, but not so easy knowing when to control your trajectory. And it required certain kinds of movement skills like chambering both hands and then thrusting them up with my palms out, just as I was about to descend.

In another exercise, you raised your elbows to prevent anyone from clipping your wings. Another set of movements was geared to the very kind of dangers I found myself facing back in the French revolution when I was in danger of being guillotined. Say a gaoler was trying to grab my hand. What Cliff taught me to do was to clamp my palm over the top of my free hand so that I could break my adversary's wrist. It was simple jiu-jitsu, but the kind of defensive move you had to learn if you ran the possibility of landing in dangerous places both in the past or future.

I had been lucky, but it's not so easy to wormhole your way out of many situations, particularly when you've blindfolded or are wearing a hood and the crowd is crying for blood.

The program recommends that you make no major changes in the first year. I had been following the suggestion ever since I got back from Camelot.

I didn't need to go back to the Big Bang to avoid the Bang Bang Club. I just had to find that place where I no longer needed to hurt others to get hard.

It was an incredibly slow process. Every time I got impatient, I tuned in with Cliff who reassured me more would be revealed in terms of love and relationships. I had to give time, time. Besides the hand techniques there are all kinds of intricacies about negotiating the fine lines between personality and time travel, where even a millisecond in the past or future can produce reparative results. There is something called "bridging," a very advanced maneuver where you literally straddle two dimensions so that you can take advantage of better DNA, without having to move from the universe you're occupying.

However, Cliff was quick to point out that this maneuver sometimes came with strings attached since it required a constant balancing act, which could expend a good deal of energy. And it is something that only experienced Worms had the skill to attempt.

Another thing Cliff worked with me on is stretching, not muscles but mind. Wormholing can be a slippery slope. A supple body has a great effect on the part of the brain that plays a role in navigating you to a universe conducive to the state of being you're seeking.

We decided to do some trial runs together. I didn't have any more sessions covered under my COBRA, but Cliff agreed to help for a little while longer anyway. I still imagined the sandwich board of the Downtown Cafe, but he showed me some of the wormholes he liked to use. We did some "behavior modification" runs in which we slipped into other dimensions in the present where my doppelganger was almost an exact duplicate of myself.

We went to one where I was attending a meeting at the Church of the Earthly Resurrection on time, and another in which I came five minutes late and missed some of the qualification. There was no shortage of possibilities. Cliff was simply trying to get me to look at wormholing like orthoscopic surgery, in which almost microscopic alterations could produce big changes.

We also did the equivalent of what civilians call "weekend getaways." We went to Vermont to see the leaves falling even though it happened to be spring. We hiked the Appalachian Trail in the dead of winter.

I would have wormholed back to my apartment after stepping into the Downtown for a burrito were it not a matter of pride. The last thing I wanted was to become one of those elderly types I'd seen at meetings who traveled through wormholes to go to the bathroom.

Once you get into the minutiae of wormholing, you see how vast the choices and problems are.

My father had always wanted to shape me up and transform me into a kind of paragon of virtue who walked the straight and narrow. Now ironically, the wormholes were enabling me to spruce up my act. I was becoming such a clean-cut young man that no one who knew me in my former life would have recognized me.

When you wormhole you have a few advantages that civilians do not, providing you're prudent in the way you manage outings. I talked a lot about Nelsa and even Muriel and what would or wouldn't have happened had I not been the person I was. What if I hadn't acted upon or even felt the urge to debase and humiliate any woman I was with in order to get it up? What if I had no trouble getting it up to begin with? Would Muriel or Nelsa and I have lived happily ever after?

Nelsa was right around the corner in time as well as space. So, she was an easy petri dish to experiment on. What would have happened between us? Would she have moved in so as not to commute to work? Would we have ended up getting married and even having kids?

Anyone who wormholes knows that, before you land, it's like opening a particularly large file on your computer. You're faced with what seems like an infinite number of choices. I stepped into worlds where Nelsa and I were fighting, where we had a family with five children, and where I had to take a civil service job for the health insurance. And there were universes where we couldn't have kids and one in which we even tried in vitro fertilization that didn't work.

I stepped into a universe where Nelsa was very fat. We fought all the time about her eating too many sweets. There was a universe in which she cheated on me. There was one I liked the most, and I almost decided to stay in it. I had won the lottery and we were fixed up for life. Of course, our problems didn't end there, since I discovered how having too much money and freedom can cause difficulties all their own, especially when it came to resisting the temptations of glitzy, fortune-hunting woman. These trophy wives are ready to do anything as long as money is involved.

In one of the alternate universes I was married to Muriel. I got a job as an insurance salesman and was quite successful. I was running an office composed of twenty associates all selling policies to Fortune 500 companies. The job entailed lots of fraternizing. I got into trouble because of an affair I had with an ambitious young ladyboy who used her charms to get on my good side. During the crisis in our marriage, we went to see a counselor who was another incarnation of Joe. We were getting relationship advice from the Marquis de Sade.

He was actually very good, though his insinuation that we might want to be more playful and inventive sexually didn't go over with Muriel, who wasn't interested in anything but old-fashioned missionary sex.

One of the points Cliff tried to make as we sailed through these "suburbs" of my personality—the locations in space/time that were near my genome—was the notion of compromise. Muriel was not someone who liked excitement. She was leery of thrill-seeking and the feeling of losing control, but she was affectionate and trustworthy and would have made a great mother.

The place where I felt the most comfortable turned out to be sitting at one of the Formica-topped tables in the Downtown Cafe, ordering the daily special from Nelsa, who placed a double-sized portion of their great guacamole on my plate.

At first, I thought I might simply have landed where we started, but it turned out that I was just a few strands of DNA away from my former self. I had to decide whether to take a chance and stay or simply go, with no guarantee I would be able to return to that same sweet spot.

It reminded me of apartment hunting. After days of looking, you finally come upon a cool possibility, but you still hesitate to sign a lease thinking something better might be right around the corner.

I felt this compulsion to decide between the life in a parallel universe with Muriel or one with Nelsa. One life seemed to afford the American dream, replete with the dog barking behind the picket fence and two cars in the garage. The other, something a bit more untidy, passionate and close to home. In fact, the only change, if Nelsa remained part-time at the restaurant in addition to working her second job as a dental hygienist, would have been to move into an apartment in the building large enough to accommodate a family.

If it weren't for the credence I had given to Cliff's advice that I wasn't ready yet, I might have made a hasty decision. In the program they always warn not to "give up before the miracle." And like a spacecraft about to land, Cliff was narrowing the territory every day—although I still felt nervous I would never be able to enjoy the pleasures of the here and now.

There were people like Jerry who simply went off to live a totally different parallel existence in some other dimension of time and space.

Cliff wanted me to hunker down in the environs of the personality I already had. It is almost like what civilians do when they see a therapist to talk about their problems, with the exception that we never specifically addressed any of my character flaws. Seeing I was coming fairly regularly, I had to have faith that he knew what he was doing.

One of the postures Cliff taught was "The Owl," a meditative stance. Your left hand is cupped within your right with the two thumbs lightly touching in the classic Zen mudra. As I visualized standing in front of the sandwich board in the Downtown Cafe, I kept my body totally still with my spine straight, as if I were a beautiful and aloof statue of the Buddha and any restless ideas were in the lives of the mortals that circled around it.

In the beginning, I was filled with big ambitions. I flailed around like someone cavorting in the waves at a beach. So, it was no wonder I landed in all those faraway places and times. More recently we'd been practicing bird-like movements that enabled me to control my trajectory. The Owl, for example, was the means by which I could affect the miniscule adjustments A final tweak revealed the ultimate secret of wormholing—*that in the end it was better not going anywhere at all.*

You couldn't arrive at this stage unless you took all the previous steps. It was something I wasn't yet ready to accept, since it meant giving up the hope of being a totally new and revamped person. However, in my heart I knew that this was where I was eventually going to land.

At the end of our last session, Cliff just winked at me.

"You know what you have to do."

Then we parted. It was raining. With the sound of a flushing toilet, I was deposited back in my apartment.

23

The Stroll

I didn't see Juanita among the ladyboys displaying their wares, but I felt a shock and quickening of my heart when I spotted Sonya, in her worn, knee-high platform boots and micro skirt, walking over as cars pulled to the curb in front of her, with the occupants rolling down their windows to haggle over prices. She was weaving and stumbling. Her thick pancake makeup, mascara and bright red lipstick failed to cover up the bruise marks all over her face. Her eyes were dilated. From the black rings, I could tell her nose was broken.

"Going out?"

Her words were slurred. I was sure she didn't even recognize me, due to my cleaned-up appearance which included removing all the studs from my pierced ears, nose and lip.

When she finally did, she staggered away.

I still felt responsible. I had to do something. Maybe some of the old timers at the meeting would have an idea about how to help.

In her desperate state, I was sure Sonya was taking some terrible beatings. Luckily, I remembered another saying I'd heard in the program: *They'll get you drunk before you get them sober.* Sonya was a great way to threaten my wormhole sobriety.

Also, as much as I didn't want to admit it, there was a small part of me that entertained thoughts of having one last fling. Someone had to help Sonya, but I realized that it was not me.

I went across the street to the diner at 11th and Second. It was filled with pre-ops but also girls from the meeting who hung out near their old stomping grounds, to keep the memories green.

"Sonya slipped," I blurted out, trying to break into the conversation.

The women closed ranks, but the one I'd been trying to talk to, a bartender with dyed black hair who worked at Webster Hall, grabbed me by the sleeve just as I turned away.

I repeated it when she said she hadn't gotten what I had to say.

"Fuck."

Looking back after I got up to leave, I could see her talking animatedly with the other women, who then looked accusingly in my direction.

Tiffany, of course, was Sonya's major sidekick, but I didn't see her.

I had some pretty good times in that dumpster on the Stroll, and I was already having fantasies about taking my belt off and tying it around Sonya's neck to make an impromptu leash—which would be mild compared to some of the other humiliations she endured. They smoked crack in those cars which were always cruising the street.

The Marquis was one of the few people who could understand my confused feelings of being tempted to take advantage of the same fallen creature I was supposedly trying help.

I was back and forth about what to do. Gwen was really just a fling. I hadn't gotten far enough to test the waters with Muriel. The closest thing I'd come to love, if that was what I had experienced, was with Lucy and that was essentially like having a relationship with a pet since, outside of the fucking, I did little more than feed her. That was what was disturbing about my fixation on Sonya. Whether guilt or desire, something drew me back to her darkness.

The Marquis de Sade and I were playing phone tag.

It was another warm spring night and the Stroll was loaded with ladyboys and ladies both, but there was no sign of Sonya. When asked if anyone had seen her, no one seemed to know who she was. There were the usual chicks with dicks flashing their tits.

Finally, I spotted her in the front seat of a white van whose driver was in the process of dumping her out onto the sidewalk. He slammed the passenger side door, his wheels spinning in some gravel as he raced off.

She was lying in the gutter, naked from the waist down, with her legs spread. I ran over, taking my jacket off to cover her.

"No," she screamed, as a crowd of streetwalkers gathered around her. "Get the fuck away from me, you piece of shit!"

Her lip was swollen and bloody and she had another black eye.

Then I was blindsided by something that knocked me out cold. I don't know if it was a rock or a fist.

I came to in the back of an ambulance. A paramedic asked me if I could follow his finger with my eyes.

"You probably have a slight concussion."

"Have you seen that girl I was trying to help?"

"You mean the one who hit you with the piece of metal pipe? Yeah, I saw her in the back of a patrol car."

I was ashamed of how horny that description still made me feel, though I was happy to see the boner now rising under the blue gurney sheet. What better proof that I was alive.

"Yeah, you couldn't help looking at her squirming as they stuffed her head into the back seat of a cruiser," he said. "She looked like she was high on molly the way she was resisting the arresting officer."

When I found out she was being booked at the precinct on East 21st, I raced over to make sure that they knew I wasn't pressing charges.

"The D.A. will get in touch with you," I was told by the desk officer, who didn't even look up at me when I explained that I was the victim of an assault.

I found out about the arraignment process and was there in court when she came before the judge. I had already dropped any charges, but she was now up for resisting arrest.

I was sure the court officer would say no when I asked if I could see her before she was remanded to talk about bail arrangements but, without batting an eye, he asked, "Are you an attorney?"

He had a large keychain hanging from his belt, and he didn't wait for my response.

I just followed as he led me to the holding cell behind the Criminal Courthouse on Centre Street.

"You have a visitor," he called to Sonya as she lay huddled in a corner.

"I don't know you!" she screamed when she saw me on the other side of the bars.

She turned away, crunching her knees against her chest in a fetal position.

The other female inmates started to call out.

"Oh, he's cute!"

"I know you, honey!"

"Looking for a date?"

"This way buddy," the officer said, poking the stick in my back when I seemed to be dragging my feet.

Well, I could always call Dial-A-Slave and simply order in. Then I would be boss again.

I finally got the Marquis on his cell.

"I feel like stripping her and leading her around the East Village on a leash. I'm in such bad shape I'm not even thinking about wormholing."

I went on to tell him about the pre-op hookers I spotted after leaving the holding cell.

"I identify," was all the Marquis had to say.

He was taciturn and aloof, but if there was one person who was going to know about S&M, it was him. He invented it.

I got a downtown 6 at 23rd and got off at Astor Place.

It was only a couple of blocks further up to the Stroll. At that time of day, the NYU undergrads who didn't like working behind the desk in the library earned pocket money by shooting up their johns. I was avoiding conjuring the sandwich board outside the Downtown Cafe, the more expeditious way of getting home. I didn't want to tempt fate. It was the sight of the Marquis himself that saved me. I saw him disappearing into the crowd filing down Eighth Street past the old Dom, which was now a meeting house for all kinds of recovery groups. I chased after his bald pate as if it were a life saver.

By the time I got to Second Avenue, he was gone. I decided I would simply head over to the Church of the Earthly Resurrection on Avenue B and sit in the pews. I didn't have my meeting list. I knew it was a safe place, where I was likely to meet the kind of people who would keep me sober, one day at a time.

I entertained the fantasy that I would walk in and find Sonya on her knees, in a good way, praying.

I must have gotten the schedule wrong. I noticed a trickle of familiar faces heading down to the dank basement space. The ceiling-high narrow windows had been painted over to keep out the light. I noticed a commotion at the speaker's desk.

"Here he is."

I didn't know her, but she plainly knew me.

"Hey Rusty, it looks like a no show. Can you chair?"

It felt like I was being asked to be the parent when I was still looking for one. Without realizing it, I'd become a fixture, the kind of person you always depend on seeing and that others look up to when they needed help or advice.

"Sure, does anyone have the preamble?"

The Marquis waved his hand in the back.

"I've asked Joe to read the preamble."

24

The Slave Auction

People at the meetings were always asking if I had a sponsor. It was their way of saying I needed help. I could have been offended, but I loved answering, "the Marquis de Sade." Seeing the look on some poor schnook's face when I said this had become a secret pleasure.

The fact was he treated all our outings as evidence. He was like a scientist collecting specimens. Even though he demonstrated a grudging respect for me now that I was a substitute chairperson at the meeting, he still exhibited an aristocratic aloofness when it came to the specter of all the suffering that humans seemed to delight in inflicting upon one another.

"Ouch, "he exclaimed sardonically as one Worm described how a crop was applied to the soles of her feet.

When you read *The 120 Days of Sodom*, you realize he has seen worse.

We agreed to get something to eat at the Downtown Cafe, but my heart sank when I saw Nelsa kissing a tall dark Hispanic-looking guy wearing a Yankees cap.

I harbored the grief at having lost my chance for the life I previewed in the parallel universe. There, I would come home from my job at the Post Office on Avenue C to a house teeming with demanding kids.

"Daddy, he pulled my hair. I imagined breaking up fights between my daughter and her delinquent younger brother who emulated his father's bad habits.

After dinner, the Marquis dipped briefly into the wormhole with me, scampering around in a few dozen alternate universes in the immediate neighborhood of my multiverse to check on the weather.

The Marquis was slightly built. His eyes prowled his surroundings, like a fox in search of its prey. Just as we were leaving, Nelsa darted outside to stop us.

"Rusty, you're going to be invited to a wedding. I'm pregnant and me and Jorge are getting married."

"Oh fuck," I whispered to the Marquis, "This is why I never wanted to feel anything."

"The lawyers are lining up" the Marquis remarked. "One door closes and another closes."

One of the problems of having a sponsor like the Marquis is that I never felt I was good enough, but as we drifted from the Big Bang back to the Bang Bang Club, I felt we were building a real sponsor/sponsee relationship.

"Any bit of quantum matter which can be in two places at the same time is a candidate for adultery." There was a gleam in his eye as he made the quip.

The Marquis drifted in and out of my vision as I floated through the wormhole. Every time I got close, he began to dissolve.

And then there were the occasional detours like the day I was sure I saw Sonya and followed her into the depths of the Bang Bang Club. It was slave auction night, and the crowd reminded me of the one I had seen outside the Old Bailey in nineteenth century London when I was nearly hanged.

I jumped when I saw Sonya buried up to her neck in garbage.

"More, more, I'm a worthless piece of shit," she screamed.

A bare-chested biker covered with tattoos and studs and wearing leather chaps with a hole in the crotch was throwing the food. As I got closer, I realized I was wrong.

I didn't see Sonya anywhere. She wasn't even in the section that contained the stocks and torture devices from puritan and medieval times.

Out of prurient interest or because I cared about Sonya and wanted to make as thorough a search as possible, I braved the line of urinals devoted to watersports, passing a poster for the annual bukkake festival in Berlin.

If Sonya were receiving a facial, I wouldn't have been able to recognize her anyway.

In their state of arousal, the crowd grew unruly. Several girls and ladyboys were being stalked by small covens intent on even more violent encounters involving spankings, slapping and pinching. I was afraid not only for Sonya's soul but her safety. What if there were necrophiliacs who wouldn't be content until they were fucking a corpse?

In the distance the ponytail of a dark-haired woman on all fours was being yanked like the reins of a horse.

I figured I would pretend I wanted to take my turn with her, and then walk her right out of the club. If she were playing the submissive role, she'd do anything I wanted, if I could pay. However, every time I tried to get near, several burly guys reminded me there was a line. I had to wait my turn if I needed to act out.

I wasn't sure if I wanted to save Sonya or fuck her in the ass, one last time. I ran back to the other room, where I glimpsed a naked woman in platform heels with her hands cuffed behind her back. She was being led down into the cellar of the club, where slaves were packed into body bags.

"Sonya, Sonya!" I yelled.

I forced my way through the mob. I shouted. It was like having one of those dreams where nothing comes out of your mouth. My cries were drowned in the mayhem of taunts and demands for more pain and humiliation, accompanied by the earsplitting thump of techno music.

25

The Union

I was running through my savings when someone from the cemetery worker's union called. They asked if I could come back to fill in for two of the regular ESL teachers who were on vacation.

When you stop hanging out all night at places like the Bang Bang Club, you have time on your hands. I leapt at the possibility to make a few bucks and get out of the house. There was no future in the job, but at least I'd have somewhere to go and something to distract me from the feelings of guilt and responsibility for Sonya.

The union hall was way out in Queens on Woodhaven Boulevard. Dan Fogarty, a red-faced Irish Catholic from Broad Channel, was still president. He was prone to fits of rage, which could be heard throughout the red brick building with its rotting, wooden "Local 9, Cemetery Workers, AFL-CIO, CWAC" sign over the facade.

My classes were sometimes interrupted by Fogarty screaming and berating his staff.

"You're a fucking dingbat," Fogarty balled, throwing a bunch of papers that had been handed to him by a quiet young man who obediently got down on the ground to pick up the mess, without a word of complaint.

"Don't you people know anything?"

"He dunno know anything," he repeated, in case nobody heard.

Now, falling into my teaching role, I found myself criticizing his grammar in the middle of these tirades.

Doesn't, I corrected, in my head.

I saw platinum-haired secretaries with old-style bouffants run from the building in tears on more than one occasion.

The union hall was his fiefdom. I was sure there was some hanky-panky involving the siphoning of dues from members, who were just happy to have their green cards, a job and a chance to take the ESL course I taught at night.

I passed Fogarty many times in the halls, but he was the kind of person who looked right through you. There were people of importance like the local Queens councilmen from the Rockaways. Then people like me. The workers who comprised his union were treated like they didn't exist.

I once heard Fogarty describe someone who was running against him in one of the rigged elections as "nothing." And if a union official was a nobody, then we drones surely occupy an even lower rung on the food chain.

Fogarty treated the cemetery workers and the employees around the hall the way I had behaved with the whores at Dial-A-Slave. So, I should have had some sympathy for him, under the theory that behind every sadist and tyrant lurks a suffering bureaucrat.

In the beginning, thirty students showed up for night school. By the next session the roster had dwindled to two who were willing to devote the time to the curriculum, which involved lots of homework.

Manuel from Ecuador was slightly built and had a winning smile. He had the sleek frame of a welterweight boxer. His body language—the way he moved his head, his eyes, his torso—made you feel he totally understood what you were saying. And maybe he did, though he didn't understand a word of English.

My other student was short and thick with wide Mayan eyes. I experienced a feeling of déjà vu when I first met Ray. I figured I encountered him when I was wormholing through ancient Mexican civilizations. He had worked his way up to foreman. He loved gardening and flowers but had been prevented from attaining a position of more responsibility because of the language barrier. He tended plots covered by "perpetual care" contracts.

The ESL classes were not high on Fogarty's agenda. There were many times when Manuel and Ray had taken a train and two buses after a long day's work, only to find that no one was teaching the class. During my previous incarnation I could be a no-show after tying one on. Now, back in the driver's seat, I made amends for my past behavior by meeting with them on evenings for which I wasn't even paid.

Fogarty had turned most of the union hall into a glorified gentleman's club replete with a dining room, bar and sauna for the union bigwigs. When Manuel, Ray and I were leaving our evening classes, we often witnessed drunken scenes. Fogarty, in his signature sharkskin suit, would drunkenly grope any women remaining on the premises.

He loved buxom broads with dyed blond hair, Marilyn Monroe impersonators who reminded me of the Elvis imitators you'd see at county fairs.

One night we even saw a couple of the Desnudas girls from Times Square with their dayglo painted breasts entering the elevator that was reserved for "union executives only."

Our classroom was in an abandoned storage closet next to the boiler room in the basement. Every time the heat cycle began, a crashing sound rattled the Board of Ed.-issue elementary school chairs with their built-in desks that were impossibly small for a grown man. As the weeks passed and word got around about the classes, the attendance again began to increase. Soon I had more students than I had tiny desks, and I had to steal metal folding chairs from the auditorium.

I wouldn't have had time to wormhole if I wanted to. Sometimes it occurred to me how odd it was having the entire universe of time and space at my fingertips, yet I ended up in a closet in the battered basement of a union hall with paint peeling from the walls. Fact was, the satisfaction of helping people turned out to be greater gratification than any of the senses I experienced travelling through all of space and time. Giving up my ego was different than getting my cock sucked in King Arthur's court. Sure, I sometimes felt a longing for the old appetites and the journeys that had enabled me to meet people like Lucy and even Sonya. But would I want to relinquish my new life helping others for fleeting pleasures that could never be satiated?

Ray dreamed of being a teacher himself and I let him start each class with the repetition of colloquial phrases.

"We're on the same page," he would drawl, and the class would respond in unison.

"Sounds like a plan…"

Ray was a bit of a joker. He'd look at me and say, "He's not the sharpest tack."

It was at this point that he would sweep his hand to the floor like a matador urging on the bull.

"El profesor!"

"Los senos" was always bound to create broad smiles on the faces of my two loyal students.

"Breasts," they intoned.

The course got some publicity in the local papers. There was even a sympathetic piece about us in the Metro section of the *New York Times* when we lost a block grant and the funding for the entire ESL program was briefly threatened.

Armed with a pile of clips, I attempted to get a meeting with Fogarty. When I called, his secretary seemed to think I was trying to sell something or shake Fogarty down. When I explained that our program came out of HR, which had no control over space in the building, her tone lightened. She set up a meeting which was promptly cancelled, as were several others.

Fogarty had a red swollen-looking nose and the air around him always reeked of rye. Finally, one Friday evening, the secretary interrupted one of my classes and said there was a window of opportunity, if I could come upstairs. I gave Ray an assignment from the workbook that coordinated with an audio disk I stuck in the boombox. Then I ascended with her to Fogarty's lair on the penthouse level.

I was led into a conference room with a long table. Fogarty sat at the end, in front of his own portrait. The room had the kind of wood paneling popular in 1970s lounges and was filled with cigarette smoke. The union president's hand was cupped tightly around a highball that even had one of those parasols you see in the TV ads for all-inclusive resorts.

"Can I get you something?" he asked, as a curvaceous redheaded waitress emerged tray in hand from the adjacent bar. She was wearing the satin *Playboy* bunny outfit with furry white tail that Hefner once used in all the clubs. Bunny ears protruded from her head. Freda Payne's '70s hit "Band of Gold" played on the jukebox standing beside a pool table.

Fogarty had been nursing his drink, now he gulped it down and held out the glass.

"Lemme have a double, Candy."

"Your life could become infinitely better." He waved at the auspicious-looking empty board table and then pointed back at his own portrait. His hand was reflected in the mirror that lay behind the built-in bar with its three leather stools.

"Yeah, you could get out of that dreary basement with the wetbacks. You'd have your own office and a girl."

For a moment I didn't know what he meant. Then I figured out that "girl" was sexist for "secretary."

I had been trying to talk to facilities about getting more desks. I never imagined I'd be meeting with the union's president. I must have looked confused since I didn't know what these promises were all about.

"We have a great health and retirement plan for all the officers here at the union while the rest of them guys are digging their own graves." He chuckled, delighted with his own humor.

I played along, trying to hide my outrage at his attitude toward the workers who were both my students and friends.

"I have a little favor I have to ask of you in exchange," he continued, as if the acceptance of his offer was already a fait accompli.

"In exchange for what?" I was about to ask. I hadn't agreed to anything. It was too bad I wasn't wearing a wire. But I didn't want to show my cards until he spewed forth exactly what he had in mind.

"Your program has gotten a lot of good publicity, which couldn't have come at a better time since the union is expanding its activities.

Into gambling, prostitution and loansharking, I thought.

"Whenever a union becomes more aggressive there's the inevitable push back from the owners. This time they've involved the feds. What we do here is business as usual. We have a little fun, but we're no different from anyone else."

"I was wondering if I could use the men's room," I interrupted. I needed a break so I could think about what I would say when he made me an offer I would have to refuse.

"Please do. You can use the executive bathroom right over there and tell Candy here to bring me another of the same," he said pointing to a silver framed doorway to heaven. "The combo is 1-2-3. Are you sure I can't get you something, a little Cabernet Sauvignon? We're supporters of the Gallo Brothers."

Candy must have overheard, as she was already sashaying into the boardroom with another highball.

The bathroom had one of those showers that can be turned into a mini steam room. I noticed a magazine rack jammed with copies of *Playboy* and *Penthouse*, and a few more of the specialized hardcore mags simply named after particular fetishes. For instance, there was one called *Gaggers* which included pictures of naked women vomiting. Another, *Barely Legal*, was hidden under a *Hustler*.

When I returned to the boardroom, a highball glass filled with a rose-colored liquid waited for me. Candy, who now joined us, was batting her fake eyelashes like they were butterfly wings

"Singapore sling," she announced.

Fogarty lifted his glass.

"Let me propose a toast to Rusty's long and fruitful relationship with our little union."

Candy raised her wine glass, which had a lipstick smudge on the rim, took a sip and then poured some coke from a small glass vial onto a coaster top, arranging it in three neat lines with a matchbook cover. She rolled a $20 bill. After snorting a line, she passed the coaster on to me. I declined, saying I had a sniffle.

"I'm worried about you, young fellow," Fogarty said as he snorted his line and then licked the coke dust from his fingers. "You know what they say in Latin? *Carpe diem*—seize the day, live for today, don't think about tomorrow."

He picked up the $20 bill. Just as Candy retrieved the vial, he motioned to her.

"Candy here thinks you're very cute," he said, winking at me and then flicking his head towards the executive bathroom as he stood up. "I have some paperwork to attend to."

Candy had the hourglass figure of an old-fashioned pinup, the kind you saw on the calendars in body shops. It was almost a parody of the old-fashioned centerfold, but like everything else at the union hall, including the worn old furniture in our classroom, she was a thing of the past. Still, I had to fight against the little tingle I felt in my crotch when, under the guise of cleaning up the drinks on the table, she bent over to the point where I could see her coffee-colored aureoles. The hidden prize laying beneath her inviting cleavage.

As I closed my eyes to pray, I felt her hands pulling down the zipper of my fly.

"Well, thanks for the drinks, Candy," I said surprised by my own ability to resist the pull of my sex addiction. "It was nice meeting you. I actually have to scoot or I'll be late for class."

"Party pooper," she said, wiping her nose.

In another life, I thought, as I pondered jumping into the wormhole for a second and simply making it all happen in an alternate universe. I took one last gander at her rack, which was as majestic as the Continental Divide, before picking up my books and papers and returning downstairs to my class.

I looked at my watch. My students would be wondering why I disappeared.

As I walked into the lobby, two men in raincoats and a third with a gun in a holster and a silver badge dangling from his neck were questioning Hansel, the pot-bellied janitor. Hansel reminded me of the soothsayer Tiresias from Greek mythology.

"Hey buddy," one of the men in the raincoats called out. He flipped open a little leather wallet which contained his badge and identification.

"I'm looking for Dan Fogarty."

When I told him I was just an ESL teacher, he handed me a

card that read "Special Agent, James Kennedy, Federal Bureau of Investigation." Below was a 347 number.

"I just saw him a few minutes ago," I replied. "He looked like he was on the way to an appointment."

For all I knew he could still have been in the building, but I realized if I said too much I'd have some explaining to do. Also, I didn't want to get Candy into trouble.

"We need to speak with him."

I thought Ray, Manuel and the others might have left, but when I got downstairs I could see that Manuel had taken over.

The students were working on commonly used phrases like "Sounds like a plan."

The one Manuel was trying out when I arrived was "We're on the same page."

The minute he saw me, he moved away from the sandwich board and returned to his seat.

"No, you're doing great," I said. "Continue on!"

He looked at me nervously. Was I an ICE agent in the guise of a teacher? Only when I opened my arms to him in a gesture of embrace did he come forward.

"I have go to the bathroom," he intoned as the class repeated the words in unison.

"Let's get trashed." I said as I walked to the blackboard.

"Let's get trashed," the class repeated.

"Sounds like a plan," I continued.

"Sounds like a plan," came the chorus of responses.

26

Bill

The headline on the Post read **UNION BOSS MISSING**. I bought a copy of the paper at the deli across the street and tucked it under my arm as I walked into the Downtown Cafe for my morning coffee and breakfast burrito.

Nelsa was already beginning to show. It was as if she were in her own alternate universe since she already looked nothing like the sexy carefree young woman I used to ogle. She was carrying more weight, not just in the literal sense, but because she had more responsibilities. The worries were written on her brow.

"You look like you going places, papi," she said, winking.

There was a touch of longing in her expression. Not for me, but for my freedom. I was single, bringing home a few bucks and unencumbered with responsibilities.

I picked up the F on Delancey.

I was planning to go in earlier to Xerox a whole new set of assignments for the class, but when I arrived at the union hall a video crew from New York 1 was lingering around the building entrance. I could see FBI agents and NYPD by the lobby bulletin board where all the notices about normal union activities, such as softball games and bowling leagues, were listed.

"Pssssp, pssssp!" Hansel waved to me from the back entrance by the dumpsters.

"C'mere," he beckoned.

I was worried about my students. If the building was on lockdown, we might not be able to meet.

We ended up having our own private little respite from the corruption investigation that was going on throughout the rest of the building. No one cared about the janitorial staff—minimum wage workers who Fogarty and his buddies had hired on the cheap precisely because they weren't members of any union. And no one seemed to know or care about the class. If they did, the cemetery workers themselves were the only ones in the union who were above suspicion.

When I saw Fogarty strutting towards me one morning on my way to work, I tried to cross the street. But he was standing right in my face before I could get away. Wearing his usual bifocals, sharkskin suit and patent leather loafers, his complexion was even more reddened than usual. He looked like he had just finished screaming at someone and was still shaking with rage. I did a double-take. Was he out on bail?

"Hey, kid." My muscles tightened as he grabbed me by the lapel. "We had some good times in the executive suite."

I had only been upstairs once, but his nostalgia had been tinged by a threat. He would drag me down with him if I didn't play ball.

"The men need me."

I was thinking that the wormhole might come in handy. I could take him back to the Inquisition or some place and leave him there.

"Don't be a snitch," was the last thing he said before disappearing into thin air.

Every day the class continued with Hansel dutifully waiting outside the union hall to usher me, Manuel and Ray into the side door. Then one day as I was about to take attendance, I noticed Manuel had brought along someone new. I figured it was just another candidate. I was ready to welcome him.

"Gonzalo Rodriguez," the visitor said, holding out his hand. "I'm the shop steward."

Though he was squat with a pockmarked face and greasy skin, I could hear right away that he spoke English with hardly any accent. He obviously had something other on his mind than ESL. Gonzalo not only spoke perfect English, he turned out to be one of those inspirational speakers who has an exceptional command of language. I even felt slightly jealous at the reverent gazes Ray and Manuel accorded him as he talked about how the union was supposed to protect the rights of the workers.

Nosotros tenemos que volver al trabajo!

"We have to get back to work," he finished, making eye contact with each of us. I couldn't concentrate. I got the idea that the union would soon be needing new leadership, but I couldn't stop thinking about Candy. My lost opportunity was calling me. I kept guiltily replaying variations on the original scene. In one, for instance, I was wresting off the bunny outfit as I pinned her down on the floor of the bathroom. The old fantasies die hard. I nodded my head sagely. When Gonzalo left, the others were able to convey the gist despite their broken English.

Apparently, my classes with the cemetery workers had turned out to be the one commendable thing that the union had done for years. And the higher-ups in the AFL were looking towards me to steward a complete overhaul of the local. Education and citizenship would be two of the important goals for members.

I had little experience with this or any union. I would have to be elected, but Ray and Manuel assured me that Gonzalo would take care of everything. Anything was better than Fogarty. At least I was honest.

Manuel and Ray both tried to explain to me that Gonzalo was a big man in union matters. If he liked me, which he appeared to, I could really go places. Maybe one day I'd even take over. Despite my lack of experience, I felt secure about the fact that I wouldn't be spending the workers hard-earned union dues on an executive bar staffed by *Playboy* bunny wannabes.

As all the garish headlines about abuses of the union coffers made the front pages of the tabloids, Gonzalo stopped by more regularly.

"This union really needs leadership, somebody new who hasn't come up through the ranks. We need to 'drain the swamp.'" He bent over and shook his head in disbelief at the other corrupt figure he was quoting, before letting out a cynical laugh.

I realized Gonzalo was moving into a position of authority. He set up a command post right next to our classroom in a small storage area, which contained cases of Fogarty's favorite drink, Seagram's Seven. I could still see that perpetually enraged scarlet face yelling for yet another "seven and seven."

Gonzalo invited me out for a drink one night after I finished class. I noticed that he only ordered a club soda with lemon as we sat at a small table in the local bar which catered to the union workers. I've never had much of a drinking problem, but ever since I started going to meetings, I stopped everything. You have a few drinks, a joint and a line or two, and before long your off to the races. I pointed to his soda and he looked at mine.

"Friend of Bill's?" he asked

"Wormhole."

"Oh, the time group...I'm a recovering alcoholic," he announced. "I've heard a lot about your meetings. I've been meaning to duck my head in, but I'm in Debtors Anonymous and I go to the sex meetings at SA. There aren't enough hours in the day."

The waitress who brought our drinks had dark watery eyes that reminded me of Nelsa's. When she bent over to put our non-alcoholic beverages on the table, I found myself staring right down into the milky white cleavage she displayed with just the right dose of demureness to excite my longing. She was obviously a good friend of Gonzalo's. When she left, he sighed and said simply, "Mariana."

I shook my head and we both laughed knowingly. In another life we would have been competing to see which of us would be first to get her into bed.

Gonzalo had most of the workers in the local ready to vote for him. He told me I commanded so much respect from the students that I had a job waiting for me, if I thought I could take another responsibility on along with the teaching.

"We don't want to lose..." he said.

The bartender must have liked the Buena Vista Social Club. As we got up to leave, she turned the volume up to a deafening level when one of their songs came on. I couldn't hear the end of Gonzalo's sentence, but I think he was complimenting me for being a "good teacher."

Mariana touched me lightly on the shoulder as we left the bar and everything in me wanted to turn back, but I just kept walking.

27

Journaling

Worms regularly engage in what's called "inventory taking." They assess the pluses and minuses of their lives and behavior. From the work point of view, I was on the way to becoming a minor official in a grave digger's local, 1258A, AFL-CIO. From the love point of view, I was celibate with no prospects on the horizon. So, I threw myself into my new work, spending most of the hours when I was not teaching advising my students about their benefits or delving into the budget of a local that was in disarray after all the years of corruption.

I'd make it home from Queens just in time to get to my evening meeting, after which I'd sometimes go out to the diner with the Marquis. I was always tempted to take the easy way home by climbing into a wormhole. However, I didn't want to be a privileged little bitch. Why shouldn't I employ public transportation like everyone else? It wasn't as if the wormhole had collapsed, though entering it week after week had definitely changed my point of view about time. What was the rush? After you've travelled back 13.5 billion years, everything becomes relative.

I hadn't taken a vacation for years, though I could have looked at my whole life before sobering up as a perpetual vacation or embarrassment or both. Occasionally, I entertained the idea of heading over to my portal, the sandwich board at the Downtown Cafe. "Seven Days and Nights in Caligula's Rome" was the kind of travel promotion that passed through my mind. A more entrepreneurial spirit might have taken advantage of his experience through history to produce packages for sex tourists, but as the old expression goes, "You don't go to a whorehouse to hear the piano player."

"People, places and things" is the way they put it in the program.

There were a couple of instances when I inadvertently caught myself staring at the sandwich board and all of a sudden started my fall from grace, before righting myself. Once I got caught up without realizing it. I stopped myself at Rome in 1962, where Pope John XXIII was giving the seventh of his eight famous encyclicals. Even though I'd played hooky from Sunday school growing up, his famous words, "We were all made in God's image, and are thus, we are all Godly alike" had always stayed with me, despite all the depredations of my life.

I tended to use the wormhole for fortune telling. It's a lot better and more reliable than having your palms read by one of those gypsies advertising in the neon-lit, second-floor windows of Hell's Kitchen taxpayers. For instance, I would intermittently be hit by attacks of guilt about Sonya. I still wanted to know how she was, though I knew I would be opening Pandora's box. I followed the Marquis's advice when he cautioned me not to go in that direction. There was a whole world of pain out there and no shortage of people who could help me by letting me help them. *I need all the help I can give* was a slogan I'd recently heard a fellow Worm share. Yet Sonya, as they said, had her own higher power.

I read that Fogarty was attributing his criminal activities to his alcoholism. He was trying to garner sympathy by announcing his attendance at AA meetings. It was an obvious ploy to beat the rap and diametrically opposed to what the program was about. I also read that Candy was subsidizing her stay at the Karen Foundation, which is a well-known rehab, by selling the rights for her story to Ed Burns, whose series *Public Morals* was just coming out on TNT.

Even though I was busier at the union than I'd ever been, I had more free time on my hands since there were neither destructive relationships nor trips though the wormholes to deal with. I signed up for a trial package at Cliff's karate dojo. The three-month membership included a Gi. Seeing that I was only taking white-belt classes, I never saw Cliff, but the dojo gave me somewhere to go when I got home from work.

I'd never known that people like the ones in the dojo existed. All the classes were totally orderly, beginning with a ceremony in which we all bowed in and acknowledged the grandmaster and the higher-ranking black belts. Then the rest of the time was spent on a series of movements that required one's undivided attention. If you came late, you have to do pushups.

Once when I was daydreaming, the Grandmaster cried out "Rusty!" and then "Makuso," which was a meditation stance in which you sit on the floor with your knees under you in a Seiza position. Everything had a consequence. Though I was humiliated at being singled out, I was at the same time astonished he even remembered my name.

Because I was a beginner, my syllabus was rather simple compared to that followed by the upper-level students. At first, I found it hard to keep up. The instructors and the Grandmaster were willing to help, but they could be harsh when you weren't doing something the right way. In karate you don't interpret; there's just one way to do things. While no one gets everything right, you're always trying to aspire towards an ideal of perfection—an ideal which is exotic to liberal-minded New Yorkers who revel in the idea that everyone should express their individuality.

I didn't know how to put this together with the tolerant atmosphere of the meetings where almost any form of verbal expression was permitted. But going to karate is like entering the wormhole in one respect: you become someone else, as least for the time you are there.

Nelsa and I had totally gotten over the bad feelings created by the abortive sex. In fact, we became close friends. I was invited to the baby shower. I always joked that I ate so many meals at the Downtown Cafe, I should get on a meal plan. Now I often found myself studying the sandwich board just for the mouthwatering specials with no idea that it might get me somewhere. Still, the program suggested that you continue the guided mediation in the wormhole, journeying to the coordinates just outside your comfort zone. You became the objective observer of your own existence. This was the closest thing to seeing a normal therapist who gave you the scoop on your behavior.

I found myself heading more and more to a little place about forty-five seconds into the past where one of my alternate selves existed like the bleed at the edge of an abstract painting. I used the other self as a palette. I watched him going to his job at the union hall. I even monitored the way this alter ego flirted with Mariana, the waitress in the bar. I kept close tabs on both my alter ego and the alter ego's alter ego, which both used the bar as a second office when they wanted to discuss things outside the confines of work.

The union hall in the parallel universe was not appreciably different from the one forty-five seconds earlier in time, which now provided the kind of health benefits that enabled me to get off COBRA for the first time in almost eighteen months. The irony was that, even though I no longer needed them, my sessions with Cliff were fully covered—as one day a week wormhole therapy was part of the new plan.

It was around this time that I started the journaling. I write down everything I do. I soon began to look at even the most insignificant events as opportunities. The average person regards a toothache or a fracas with their significant other or a ticket for jaywalking—like the one I received from an overly zealous rookie cop as I bee-lined across First Avenue—as an annoyance. No one likes it when your order of take-out Chinese is missing the delicious little bags of crunchy fried noodles.

"You want cold sesame noodles?"

"No, I just want one of those little plastic bags with the crunchy noodles."

These kinds of exchanges are grist for my mill. Since I started living a sober way of life, I no longer have any real calamities. But I welcomed the little mishaps that do occur so I could write about them. It wasn't worth going to court to fight my jaywalking fine, but I had a vignette for my journal. I barely said a word to Mariana, but I'd written pages about her. Had I embarked on a lurid affair, I might have been so obsessed with what our next sex act would be that I might not have been able to imagine her and create the character who was now developing in the little spiral notebook, which fit in the back pocket of my jeans.

Whatever I do now seems to have a meaning. I was as gluttonous for things to write about as I once was for sex. I didn't like it when I got a fever or a cold or eat too many of my beloved burritos at the Downtown Cafe, but everything became fodder. Most people simply slog through the difficult periods of their life, waiting for them to pass, hoping that someday their fortunes will turn and things will get better. But now even the question of my erections or lack thereof was a subject to write about. The downside, if there was one, was that I never really enjoyed things or participated in them as they occurred— as I was the observer of my own existence. Gonzalo and I had lots of meetings. Along with the cleanup after years of fraud, everyday matters like negotiating the cemetery workers three-year contract and making sure they were getting a graduated set of wage increases from one year to the next, plus all the benefits, had to be ensured. I naturally took notes about what occurred. I always had a notebook out. While I was recording the conversations, I was recording the very act, as if I were writing about a character in a book, an addictive personality who was now in recovery and working for a union that protected the rights of gravediggers.

I wrote down my guided meditations in the wormhole. This was just like jotting down the contents of a dream, but now whenever I tried to look down the half-unbuttoned blouse of some hottie, I turned the negative energy into a story. My fantasies become the fuel for my writing. Instead of trying to squelch and repress them, I now had a way they could be freely expressed.

Striking woman, model's looks, tall, thin, beautiful skin, penetrating eyes, aquiline nose wearing long gray wool dress, accentuating figure, calf-high boots, hair pulled back in tight bun, not distracted or aloof, totally demure, almost vulnerable, innocent yet seductive, ingénue and sexual adventurer.

Rather than futilely trying to make eye contact with what was essentially a phantom of my imagination, I continued to write. I found myself scribbling down impressions feverishly while my latest subject sat at the other end of a subway car, even if she never looked in my direction. That's one of the wonderful things about journaling. You can totally record your observations without anyone having to know about it. Sure, I occasionally looked up to correct an impression. Was she wearing a red or green silk scarf? However, these are the kinds of things I could take in from the corner of my eye.

If I had done my usual and succeeded in fulfilling my mantra, "a beautiful face to debase," I would have written a far more linear and predictable story, ending the way most of my sexual experiences had with the horrified recipient of my aggression grabbing their clothes off the floor and fleeing as fast as possible from the site of his or her degradation. In this one, my subject was a romantic fantasy come to life.

Model for Picasso, Matisse. One day her likeness simply walks out of the Prado. She becomes the lover of a famous blind Argentinian writer, who uses her as the basis for stories. Eventually she escapes to New York where her aristocratic and well-kept appearance only camouflages the poverty of her existence. She speaks little English and uses the subways for shelter, getting food from soup kitchens on the Upper East Side.

Her image is still missing from the painting. Even though she's been a prisoner of the artwork, there are times when she longs for the love and adulation accorded in her former incarnation in the portrait.

Before I got off at Grand Central, where I would change for the downtown 6, I jotted down all my notes for the story. When I looked up, as the doors of the train opened, she was already gone.

It was early October. There had been a hurricane warning. The latest threat, Wilhelmina, which had lashed the Bahamas with 90 mph winds, reminded me of wormholes. Dark clouds hung over the city. Strong gusts blew heavy sheets of rain across the streets. It was the kind of day filled with inconveniences for most people, but which provided me with more things to write about.

I don't watch much TV, but I almost look forward to storms since I love to watch the coverage on the Weather Channel. It is the one remnant of my sadistic desire to see other people suffer. There I was in my cozy little fifth-floor apartment while the streets of some town on the Jersey Shore like Asbury Park or Margate were slammed with water levels that flooded the highways and bring traffic to a halt.

It was during the weekend of that storm that I conceived the title for the novel I was going to write about my life, *The Wormhole Society*. It wouldn't be one of those *bildungsroman* I'd read about. It wouldn't be a novel of psychological development, but it would definitely be autobiographical to the extent that it would be all about me, right up until the so-called present. After all, what else did I know about? Since it would involve the wormholes, which could also be like typhoons in the way they uprooted you, it would read like science fiction. Unlike most autobiographical novels, it would tell the history of not only the world, but the creation of life itself.

While I still didn't know what love was, I now had a project that I was passionate about and which I leapt into every morning before I went to work.

I wasn't satisfying the pleasures of the senses and sometimes I felt like one of the Zen monks who practiced Kung Fu in the Shaolin Temple—a place which has a sacred importance to martial arts practitioners. But I had a life. Whenever I felt the longing for the excesses of the past, I knew I could write about them. In fact, whether I liked it or not the first pages of my novel turned me on as I wrote them down.

I got to relive the Stroll and the first time I called up Dial-A-Slave. Sometimes sitting in my living room, watching the evening news and looking around at the ordered shelves of books, the CD player with its neatly placed speakers, and the freshly swept floors, I couldn't believe that the chaos I was writing about had ever occurred.

My biggest problem was the character of Sonya. My last memory was seeing her eyeballs practically going back up into her head with paramedics and policeman surrounding her. Then there was the prim and proper Sonya with her head covered by a scarf, the warm and loving Mother Teresa who spent her life helping others. People who worked the Stroll and shot coke with their johns, as I was certain Sonya had been doing at the end, OD'd all the time. I wasn't sure if I wanted to write about the character I had known or the person who had an awakening—the person I wished her to be. In writing, like wormholing, you can make big or little adjustments that change a person's story.

Writing is very much like cruising though my life while at the same time keeping my distance from it. When I write, I look down on myself the way I did when I was hovering over an alternate universe. I am viewing my own existence as if I were someone else. The difference is that the person I am seeing is not some variation of myself but the person I had always been.

I'd learned a lot from wormholing.

I was a devoted member of my group, but I increasingly had less use for the wormholes themselves. Billie Holiday sang "Ghosts of yesterday/knocking on my door…" There was something haunting and even frightening about the idea of my alter ego cruising through the holes and peering into all the strings and time/space coordinates, the hidden nooks and crannies surrounding the real life I was born into. I no more wanted to journey into another wormhole than delve into the dark cellar that housed the Bang Bang Club. I began to feel I might no longer be able to descend into a wormhole, even if I wanted to. I'd lost the gift of desperation—what we called "GOD" at meetings—that often fueled these excursions.

There is an adult bookstore up the block from my apartment, the kind of place that displays cheap women's lingerie in the windows along with dusty secondhand S&M DVDs of guys wearing leather chaps with no bottoms. There was a basement area with booths. I watched the clientele coming in and out over the years.

I don't have any regrets about the sleazeball I have been, and the itch I still feel as I watch the store's traffic is like one of those little blips where I briefly journeyed back and found myself with Sonya on the floor of the apartment.

I always returned happy to be alive and freed from my compulsions. *You have to pay* runs through my mind as I watch a wino stumbling on the curb, but just as the guilt is about to hit, I hear *if those things hadn't occurred you would never have developed a spiritual life.*

I had never bought the idea that there is an order and purpose to the universe and that, as some people at the meetings like to say, I would become the person I was meant to be. But there is no doubt that I, Rusty Russianoff, is a union official and sometime writer.

One Monday morning, I went to the Downtown Cafe for my usual café con leche before walking up First Avenue toward the subway when I stopped right in my tracks. The face was familiar, but I couldn't place it right away. Then, turning around, I recognized the woman with the petite features hidden behind a mane of long blond hair.

It was right after Thanksgiving, which I had spent at Gonzalo's home with his wife and three kids. The kids took to me. I felt like a long-lost uncle. It was a taste of domesticity that I wasn't entirely prepared for and that also created a touch of claustrophobia. The first Xmas lights were just being strung up above the bodegas and pharmacies and in a few places across the Avenue itself. The light snow that had been falling melted on the sidewalk. My new black Converse were already getting wet from the slush.

"Rusty!"

I didn't recognize her at first. Then I remembered the *Post* headline, **BATTERED PROSTITUTE FOUND IN MIDTOWN HOTEL**, which I'd read as I stopped at a Pakistani news store. Suddenly everything went quiet. I was paralyzed by fear and guilt. I envisioned a headline about Sonya's naked body being discovered in a dumpster.

"It's Tiffany."

The spiked hair of the lesbian punker was gone along with the piercings on her nose, ears and cheek. She'd turned back into one of those all-American types you find on the tennis court in Greenwich. But it turned out to be Chappaqua.

"Susan Fairfax," she said, holding out her hand in a business-like fashion. "This is Missy." She pointed to a toddler in a ballet tutu and slippers, who averted her eyes as I stared down at her.

"We're on our way to Gymboree."

My instinct was to pretend I didn't recognize her and continue walking. I was on my way to work so I had an excuse ready if she asked to get coffee. Whatever her tale was, I almost didn't want to hear it.

"We're actually late, c'mon Missy," she said, tugging the little girl along like a rag doll, as I stood there without responding. "Good luck, Rusty!"

Panic overcame me as we turned away from each other. I feared I had lost my last connection to the past and to Sonya. The rush-hour crowd, heading towards the subway at Union Square carried me along. The concern with Sonya was mixed with the sediment of my old desires. Sonya herself was a kind of black hole, in which I could still lose my footing. *Look back don't stare* is another phrase bandied about in the rooms. However, on a moment's impulse I gave into temptation and made an about-face. I ran as fast as I could down First Avenue.

I was thrilled when I spotted Tiffany's mane of blond hair and sensible patent leather pumps. I remembered she walked on the balls of her feet. She always looked like she was falling over herself. It was her signature gait. But when I ran up from behind, crying out "Tiffany!... I mean Susan!" and grabbed her sleeve, a strange woman turned around with a remonstrative look on her face. She shook me off like I was one of the aggressive homeless types hooked on synthetic weed who accost people on the avenue.

I stood paralyzed in the middle of the sidewalk, impervious to the blur of humanity that was passing me by.

28

Fries

I got a call from the Marquis. He told me Sonya was alive. She stabbed one of her tricks with a pen and ended up on Riker's.

A few of us from the meeting chipped in. She ended up in a rehab instead of having to do hard time. So, it was I who was now doing the reforming rather than being reformed.

One of the things that had been holding up the writing was what I was finally going to do about the character of Sonya. I couldn't just leave this loose thread. Readers would want to know what happened, regardless of whether *The Wormhole Society* was regarded as science fiction or not.

You can humiliate a character in a novel, but it's a far cry from trying to get your kicks by hurting somebody you meet in in a bar or sex club like the Bang Bang. Now I knew her fate.

As I rode to work in the morning, I assiduously made notes not only about the people in the subway cars, but about the characters in *The Wormhole Society*, which is to say all the people who I met in all the alternate universes I inhabited.

I spoke with Sonya over the phone several times while she was in the rehab. My awareness of being a force of good in her life now aroused feelings of love, the kind of love you feel towards someone you want to rescue and protect. Soon after she was released, we agreed to meet.

I felt anxiety in the pit of my stomach as I got closer to the Belgian frites joint on Second Avenue, which had become my new go-to place (now that I was avoiding the sandwich board of The Downtown Cafe), despite the altercation and beating I endured there during my other life.

There were undoubtedly parallel universes where Sonya continued on her path of destruction. I could see the image of her mangled limbs protruding from a pile of garbage, all but unidentifiable except for the worn knee-high leather boots along with the micro-skirt she wore when prowling the streets.

I shuddered, wondering if she had ever been a mark for serial killers like Joel Rifkin who haunted the very Lower East Side streets Sonya had walked.

She was late. I waited by the window anxiously, thinking I was kidding myself. I was convinced she didn't share my feelings. In fact, it was possible she still maintained the same animosity. There was a bus stop right outside the window. Each time one would unload, my face would grow hot. I could hear my heart thumping. Now forty-five minutes later, I figured she was a no-show.

Sonya had a chameleon-like appearance anyway. Her hair could be dyed jet black, purple or even flaming red. She was like a butterfly or praying mantis who was able to hide by of camouflaging her real self. It was work to locate her face. I flinched when the strange woman in the female version of old-fashioned motorcycle boots approached through the cloud of smoke created by a new batch of fries the chef was just beginning to salt.

The mixture of her changed appearance, which now included a totally new mohawk style hairdo, caught me off guard. I felt a rush of love and immediately opened my arms to her in a way I never had before.

It was only when we pulled away from each other that I realized she wasn't alone. She was in the company of the very guy I had scuffled with that first time. I was now repeating the first scene of *The Wormhole Society*—only this time I wouldn't be reaching for anyone's fries.

I could see my old adversary remembered me and was intent on taking up where we left off. When the Dominican counter guy handed me the cone of fries I ordered, the punk brazenly dug in to help himself. He was determined to show me how it felt— before we'd even been introduced.

I clenched my fists. I owed him one.

I realized that Sonya's choice of the similar style was like an exchange of wedding bands.

"Dizzy's one of us. He goes to meetings," Sonya said, looking meaningfully in both our directions. She didn't realize it, but the disclosure had stopped me just as I was about to lunge.

More like one of you, I thought.

"Rusty and I go back."

"Any friend of Sonya's..." he began sarcastically, as I muttered "Cut it, pal" under my breath.

I wasn't sure if I wanted to write or live what was going to happen, though I knew I didn't have much of a choice unless, of course, I was going to rush back into the wormhole.

I was hurt. I hadn't realized how much I'd pinned my hopes on the possibility of us becoming an item. But at least I was feeling something, which itself was progress.

I didn't want to participate in their conversation, which was mostly composed of the kind of shorthand and accompanying body language that people use when they are in a relationship. In any case, this was plainly just a pit stop for them.

Sonya tied a scarf around her neck, then kissed me. I touched the spot and then brought my fingers to my nose as if to savor, if only for moment, the smell of her flesh.

I didn't say anything when they both started to leave. I must have looked lost.

"Are you OK, Rusty?"

In the here and now.

"I'm fine."

I watched from my perch as they fearlessly crossed Second Avenue, even as the ongoing traffic bore down upon them.

www.ingramcontent.com/pod-product-compliance
Lightning Source LLC
LaVergne TN
LVHW091546070526
838199LV00023B/553/J